A DOORWAY THROUGH TIME

Sequel to *A Doorway Through Space*
Winner of Mayhaven's Award for Children's Fiction

Judith Bourassa Joy

Mayhaven Publishing, Inc.
803 E Buckthorn Circle
P. O. Box 557
Mahomet, IL 61853
USA

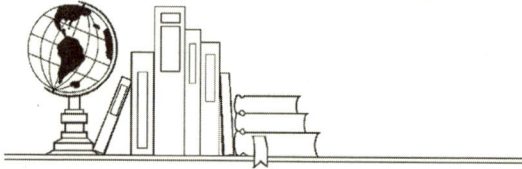

Cover Design: Zachary Lane
Cover Art is a composite painting
created by the participants of the Charleston, IL TEENReach program
with the assistance of the Coles County, IL, Arts Council
Copyright © 2014 Judith Bourassa Joy
Library of Congress Cataloging Number: 2014953565
First Edition—First Printing 2014
ISBN 13: 9781939695246
ISBN 10: 1939695244

Dedication

✿ ✿ ✿

"It is a thin membrane that separates
the temporal from the eternal."

To the power of family ties,
the marvels of science, and
the gifts of laughter and imagination,
in loving memory of Judy

Judith Bourassa Joy
July 17, 1964—November 12, 2013

Chapter 1
⚜ ⚜ ⚜

"Terrorists Destroy Spaceship!" Lucy stared at the headline on the news article, then glanced at the story's filing date: April 1, 2064.

April Fool's Day, she thought. *That was some bad cosmic joke.*

She sighed and slowly scanned the article again, even though she had memorized its contents long ago.

"The space transport *Icarus* exploded en route to Mars this morning. Green Planet terrorists, opposing the colonization of other planets, have claimed responsibility for the nuclear blast. The ship's black box, which was encased in two-inch lead lining, recorded that the *Icarus* was completely destroyed. The eight-member crew had no time to launch an escape pod. Those killed included Captain Jason Knowles, Chief Engineer Henry Starrett..."

At this point, Lucy grimaced and shut her eyes. "Close," she whispered, and when she opened her eyes, the news file was no longer in sight.

Lucy murmured, "Open family album. July 2058."

Lucy's view of her bedroom disappeared as her contact lenses transitioned to display an opaque image from her 10th birthday party. She smiled to see her younger self, trying out her first hoverboard. Her father, Henry, looked almost as excited as she did. Lucy remembered how anxious he was to try the board for himself. In the end, Lucy's mother, Ellen, purchased a hoverboard for him, too.

Lucy flicked her eyes to the right to page through other images, several of which documented the hoverboarding excursions she had enjoyed with her father.

"July 2062," Lucy ordered.

The next image was of Lucy's 14th birthday. The day was marked by a special gift from her brother, Donald. He was handing her a pet rat, a tiny puff of white fur she named Bentley, who grew into a large, handsome rat that had played an important role in Lucy's recent mission to the planet Tairran. Lucy felt her throat tighten at the sight of her beloved pet. He had died just a few weeks earlier. *At almost three years old*, she told herself, *he had a pretty long life for a rat. And he had a great life, too.*

She continued flicking her eyes to the right, quickly paging through the months until she paused at Christmas 2063. It was a rare formal portrait of her family, arranged by a professional photographer. A huge, decorated tree could be seen in the background. Lucy's father and mother were seated in the center, which made it difficult to appreciate the height difference between her tall, fiery-haired father and her tiny, dark-haired mother. Lucy and Donald stood flanking their parents.

Lucy absent-mindedly twirled a strand of her long red-gold hair around her finger as she studied the image. *The photographer was right to separate me from Donald*, she thought. *It's not so obvious that I'm taller than my 'big' brother.*

Although Lucy was a confident teenager, she was still often uncomfortably aware that her six-foot height set her apart from most of her peers.

A sudden twinge of pain in her forehead made Lucy sit bolt upright on her bed. She knew it signaled the onset of an "extrasensory moment," as their close family friend Dr. Hartwick termed it.

A year earlier, Lucy's mother had captained a ship that disappeared at the same point in space where the *Icarus* had been destroyed. Lucy, Donald, Dr. Hartwick, and a military cadet named Scott Davenport had embarked on a rescue mission that took them through a wormhole to the planet Tairran—4.2 light years from Earth. It was during these travels that Lucy discovered her gift for telepathy. Until then, headaches had simply been something to be endured, but on Tairran they were the precursor to Lucy's ability to communicate telepathically.

Lucy had not used her telepathic skills since she'd returned to Earth, though she found she had a heightened sense of intuition and could often read the emotions of others. She now sensed a strong feeling of anxiety emanating from her mother. She squeezed her eyes shut long enough to clear her contact lenses and then raced downstairs. She slowed to a tiptoe as she approached the kitchen, then gently pushed the swinging door ajar. She peered around the opening and saw her mother speaking with two people on the videophone—her Uncle Marcus and Aunt Rhea.

Oh no, Lucy groaned.

Marcus and Rhea were two of Lucy's least favorite people, mainly because of their bothersome twin sons, 11-year-olds Romi and Remi. No one in Lucy's family liked the twins, who were known for their destructive practical jokes.

Rhea was speaking rapidly, "Romi was just saying how much he misses his Aunt Ellen and cousins Lucy and Donald."

Lucy pressed her hand against her mouth to suppress a laugh.

"How... sweet," Ellen replied.

Lucy looked closely at her aunt's olive skin, straight nose, and mass of dark hair, loosely bound up so that long curls escaped and cascaded down her neck. She pictured her aunt as a statue of a Greek goddess, which seemed perfectly appropriate as Rhea was a well-known Latin professor and a scholar of Greco-Roman mythology.

Rhea's dark eyes were pleading now.

A Doorway Through Time

What does she want? wondered Lucy.

"Look here, Ellen, it's just for four weeks, until the nanny returns from her damned inconvenient holiday," interrupted Marcus in clipped accents. "I know you'll be on some team-building retreat for that space agency of yours, but if you can drag along Lucy, then surely nobody would mind a couple of strapping young boys running about as well. You know that if you'd gone and gotten yourself blown up like Henry, we would've taken your children in a heartbeat."

Ellen winced, and Rhea looked away.

Rhea's ashamed of her husband, Lucy realized. *As she should be.*

Lucy felt her mother's struggle to control her anger.

After a moment, Ellen directed her hostility at Marcus, "You know perfectly well that's a ridiculous argument. I *did* disappear a year ago, and my daughter and son managed just fine on their own. Better than fine, as you well know. And since we're being brutally honest, if Lucy and Donald had needed a home, I wouldn't have wanted them staying with you. You and Rhea are always traveling the globe. Instead of trying to save the world, maybe you should try to save your own family and stay home with your children for once."

Marcus's face turned red, then purple. "Fine!" he shouted. "We'll make other arrangements! Come along, Rhea," he called over his shoulder as he disappeared from view.

But for once, Rhea didn't dutifully follow her husband. Lucy was surprised to see tears forming in her aunt's eyes.

"Perhaps you're right, Ellen, but I know that Marcus needs me," she whispered. "Please, what Romi says is true. You're our closest relatives and the boys really are fond of you, even if they don't show it. Next summer... next summer, I swear we will spend the holiday with our sons. But it's too late to change plans now. Marcus is needed to consult on a project that will help Indonesian tsunami victims rebuild their homes."

Lucy felt her mother's conflicted emotions of sympathy and annoyance. Sympathy won out.

"Very well, Rhea," Ellen replied, clearly irritated. "I'll take your sons with me to Italy. But I warn you—if you don't keep them with you next summer, I will never bail you out again. Those children need their mother and father."

"Oh, thank you," Rhea cried with relief. "I will tell Marcus and the boys the good news right now! You will see my angels in one week's time!"

"Wait, when exactly—?" began Ellen. But it was too late. Rhea had ended the videophone connection.

Lucy burst through the kitchen doorway to confront her mother.

"What do you mean, 'I'll take them with me to Italy'?

A Doorway Through Time

Aren't you going to be spending your days working on that top-secret time machine with Dr. Hartwick and his team?"

"So you saw the whole thing?" asked Ellen. "Yes, of course you must have sensed my... strong feelings about your father's brother and his wife."

Ellen drew herself up to her full five-foot height and looked her daughter squarely in the eye. "Yes, Lucy, I'm afraid I am going to be very busy with my work. Marcus and Rhea think I'll be on a business retreat. But as you know, I couldn't get us out of this one—this time. I'm afraid that during the day, while I'm at work, you're going to have to take charge of the little demons... ah... darlings."

"But what about Scott? You know I was planning to invite him to join us, since Donald can't go."

"Then he can help you, and the odds will be in your favor. Two tall and capable grown-ups—" Ellen dramatically tilted her head up to appraise Lucy's six-foot height— "against two little boys."

"Yeah right," Lucy muttered. "You're just saying that because you're outrageously short. It would take a small army to stack the odds in my favor. Those kids are a menace to society."

Ellen leaned back against the kitchen counter and folded her arms. "Listen to me, Lucy Ellen Starrett. It's too late for us to back out now, so we just have to make the best of it. Those kids have a poor excuse for a family, so we're going to be their family all of four weeks. I'm sure anyone who can steal a spaceship, go through a wormhole, convince a planet full of aliens that she's a goddess, and rescue her mother, can handle baby-sitting two young boys for a few weeks."

Lucy took one look at her mother's face. She didn't need to use any special powers to realize that this was the end of the conversation.

"Whatever," she replied in the most offended tone she could muster. "I'd better go talk to Scott."

Lucy went straight to her room, grabbed a brush, and hastily tugged it through her hair. She checked herself in the mirror, considered changing her clothes, and then decided against it.

This is ridiculous, she thought. *It's just a call to an old friend. Still...* Her heart was pounding as she spoke the command, "Contact Scott."

Her anxiety dissipated as soon as Scott's image appeared on the screen. He flushed with pleasure, and broke into a wide grin.

"Lucy!" he nearly shouted. "What's up? Did you remember that today I'm finally free? I just finished my final exams, and I don't have another officer training assignment until fall."

"That's great, Scott. Congratulations! In fact," she hesitated for a second, "I'm actually calling to invite you to join me on a family trip for a month this summer—to Italy!"

A Doorway Through Time

"Whoa, Italy?" replied Scott. "I'd love to! It'll be you, me, your mom and Donald?"

"Not exactly," Lucy answered hesitantly. "I'm afraid Donald's going straight from MIT to a summer internship at Aeronautics International, so he can't come. I hope you don't mind."

"Why would I mind as long as you're there? I mean, of course it's too bad Don can't come—you know, I'll miss him, but, well..."

He wants to see me most of all! Lucy realized.

"I know what you mean. I'll miss him, too. But I'm so glad you can come. It seems like forever since I've seen you." She took a deep breath and then continued. "But Scott, I haven't told you everything. My 11-year-old cousins have to join us. It's a long story, but their parents are going away for a few weeks, and they need someplace to stay. And—I have to keep an eye on them during the day. Do you mind terribly?" Lucy finished in a rush, "We could still go out on our own at night."

"Oh." Scott looked a little taken aback at first, then grinned. "Hey, that's no big deal. I'd be glad to help you. How hard can it be to take care of two little kids? It's not like they're in diapers."

"Believe it or not, babies would be a lot less trouble. I'm afraid these boys are super-smart and super-obnoxious. A few years ago, they found my old stuffed animals in my closet. They gutted every one and dumped the stuffing all over my room. Last winter, they found my middle-school diary and put it online! Can you imagine? Then they lit all the candles in my room, and one of my curtains caught fire."

"Maybe it's just you they like to torment," answered Scott with a wicked grin.

"Hardly," Lucy groused. "They've outworn their welcome at plenty of places. Most of the time, they're so bad their mother has to retrieve them early. At my cousins' house, the twins did all the classic pranks, like putting sugar in the salt shaker and salt in the sugar bowl. They put plastic ants in the cereal and fake vomit on the living room rug. Then they reprogrammed all the keys. No one could start the hovercars, and my aunt got locked out of the house in a snowstorm—wearing only her bathrobe and slippers! That did it. They got sent on the next plane back to their parents who, I think, were in Brundi, that time."

Lucy looked down, suddenly very nervous. "So it's okay if you don't want to come after all. I mean, I probably wouldn't either, if I were you."

"Lucy, look at me," Scott said quietly.

Hesitantly, Lucy raised her eyes to meet his, worried about what she might see there.

"Lucy, will you be there?"

Confused, Lucy replied, "Well, yes. Of course."

"Then that's all that matters."

Chapter 2

ᨡ ᨡ ᨡ

The next week passed in a blur of activity. Lucy offered to take care of closing up the house for the summer so that her mother could focus on her work. She was surprised at how much effort that took. She adjusted the home's temperature controls, recalibrated the pool's automatic cleaning and chemical dispensing programs, set the mower to cut the grass once every ten days, and programmed the robo-maid to dust and vacuum every two weeks. She did all the laundry. She emptied and washed down the refrigerator and freezer. Hardest of all was trying to decide what to pack for an eight-week sojourn to Italy. After studying five years of weather trends for the remote central Italian region to which they were heading, Lucy decided on an assortment of her lightest summer clothing. She also downloaded a selection of new books and magazines to her reader, packed some sketch paper and colored pencils, and at the last moment, stuffed her hoverboard into her largest bag.

After all, it sure was useful on my last trip. Not that I'm expecting to conquer another alien civilization. She grinned at the thought.

At the end of the week, Lucy drove to the airport to pick up Scott. Late as usual, she anxiously scanned the info-column in the baggage area for arrival information.

Oh no, she thought, *his flight landed 20 minutes ago. He's probably wondering if I forgot.*

Suddenly, a shooting pain in her forehead made her gasp and stumble.

Don't worry, a voice in her head interjected. *Your boyfriend is on the escalator, looking for you.*

Who's there? Lucy wondered, *and how did you get in my head?*

Glancing up, she saw Scott at the top of the escalator. For a moment she was breathless, distracted by his handsome features and broad smile. She waved frantically until she caught his eye.

Recalling the mental intrusion, Lucy began looking about.

Calm down, my dear. I got into your head the same way that you got into mine. You're not the only telepath around, you know. As for my identity, look to your left, next to the info-column.

Lucy turned around. The display on the column was changing now, dissolving from an arrival list to a chart of

16

international time zones. Just below the current time in London, Lucy saw her—an exotic woman with mocha-colored skin was nodding toward her. She was dressed in a flowing, multi-colored gown and a large, saucer-like hat.

Are there many people like us? Lucy wondered as she made her way through the crowd.

I imagine there are quite a few. There are certainly many people with stronger intuition than others. How else could mediums and psychic police investigators do their jobs?

I didn't realize they were for real, Lucy confessed. *I guess it doesn't make sense that I'd be the only telepathic human on Earth.*

Lucy felt a light pressure in her head, and it took a moment to realize her memories were being probed. She quickly closed her mind.

Very good, Lucy. You know how to protect your thoughts. But I sense—and I briefly saw—that there was something more behind your words, 'the only telepathic human on Earth.' I do believe you have traveled to other planets. And because I don't live under a rock, I think you must be Lucy Starrett, the inter-galactic space heroine the news was so full of last year.

Lucy flushed and nodded.

Now you are far more interesting to me, Lucy, since I know you are one of us, continued the woman. *You see, you just needed to meet another humanoid with powers like your own in order to communicate. And true telepaths are a bit more unique. I belong to a network of telepaths in the northeast region of the United States. There are 12 of us registered. If you were to join our society, you would bring our number to lucky 13.*

Lucy had reached the woman now, and she took the hand extended to her. Lucy's own hand tingled with electricity when their palms touched. When she was released from the handshake, Lucy found a business card in her hand:

Sayesha Herero
Medium, Psychic, Telepath
Member, PT
(Psychics & Telepaths)
Available by appointment.
References provided.
U101-1313-1313
sherero-uverso

"You're right—I am Lucy Starrett. I'm very glad to meet you, Sayesha," said Lucy aloud.

"Am being glad to meet you," came the halting reply. "My English is not so good, but my telepathy is fantastic," Sayesha added slowly. *Think about it, Lucy. We would be glad to have you join us. I would like very much to correspond with you. Would that be all right?*

A Doorway Through Time

Lucy nodded. "I would like to know you better, Sayesha."

And now—your boyfriend is right behind you.

He's not really my boyfriend, thought Lucy.

Lucy turned and hurried to a smiling Scott. She quickly scanned his six-foot plus frame, his thick, sandy blond hair, and his deep blue eyes. *As handsome as ever*, she thought.

Scott extended his arms, and Lucy felt as though she would melt as he hugged her.

"I'm really glad to see you, Lucy," he said as they stepped back from their embrace. "I've missed you."

"I've missed you, too," Lucy replied. "A lot. And I'm sorry I'm so late."

"You, late? How unlike you," Scott joked. "But don't worry, I just got here. It took forever to get off the plane. An old lady ahead of me failed her optical identity scan."

"Was she a criminal?" Lucy asked, incredulous.

"No, she'd just grown some cataracts since she registered her last scan. Hey—I see my bags coming! Let's get out of here."

Scott started toward the baggage claim when Lucy put a hand on his arm.

"Wait, Scott, before you go, I'd like you to meet a new friend of mine—Sayesha Herero."

She turned back toward the column, but Sayesha had vanished.

Are you out there, Sayesha? Lucy called telepathically.

I'll see you later, came a faint reply. *And that's a promise. But right now, you need time with your boyfriend.*

But he's not my... oh, forget it.

Lucy noticed Scott staring at her. "You have a funny look on your face, Lucy. What's wrong?"

"I was just talking to Sayesha—telepathically."

Lucy anticipated Scott's next question. "She can't speak English very well, so we talked telepathically. It turns out there are telepathic societies all over the country!"

She handed Sayesha's business card to Scott. He examined it in silence.

"Scott, Sayesha invited me to join the northeast region group. I have a really good feeling about her. I just might join..." she trailed off.

"Let's get to the car, Lucy, and you can tell me more."

They grabbed his bags and hurried off to the hovercar, chatting about Sayesha and then inconsequential news until they got to the parking tube. The tube was a metallic structure, twenty stories high. Lucy walked up to a garage-sized door and punched in her parking code. There was a grinding sound as gears churned.

"Sorry, Scott, it's on the nineteenth level," Lucy apologized.

"No problem, Luce."

They watched as the light display showed the hovercar's slow progress down the tube. Finally, the door opened with a hiss, and the hovercar slid out of the bay. An electronic voice echoed out from the garage.

"$175.00 has been charged to your account."

"Wow, the rates went up again!" Lucy exclaimed. "Good thing it's Mom's account and not mine. She's going to get her money's worth out of our baby-sitting services, though."

Lucy and Scott climbed in and drove out of the airport. Lucy merged onto the lowest level of the airway, concentrating on making her way upward through the vertical layers of traffic.

"Scott, can you see if anyone's coming above me?" Lucy asked.

Just then a sporty red hovercar zoomed by overhead.

"He must have been doing 250!" Scott exclaimed in annoyance. "What a jerk!"

"Maybe I'll just stay on the third level," Lucy decided. "These city drivers are crazy."

They were quiet for a minute as the hovercar sped silently along its airway. Scott broke the silence.

"I meant it, Lucy, when I said I'd missed you."

Lucy looked at him. "Did you keep your part of the bargain? Did you date girls at college?"

"I did. And did you date any high school guys?"

"Yeah, a couple..."

Scott flinched. "It was awful!"

"Terrible!" Lucy agreed. They both began to laugh.

"The boys in high school just seem so immature to me now. After all you and I went through, it's hard to care whether or not the soccer team makes it to the state finals."

"I know what you mean. The girls I dated were boring compared to you. They agreed with everything I said."

"Hey—" Lucy interrupted.

"And they were nowhere near as beautiful," Scott finished.

Lucy blushed. "So the experiment is..."

"Over," replied Scott. "We've tried dating people our own age, and it didn't work. I'm not going to find someone else, no matter what you think. I'm only a couple of years older than you, Lucy. It's not such a big difference. And I think we can make a long-distance relationship work. I really don't think your mother will mind. I know Donald approves, because I just talked to him about it yesterday."

"You talked to Donald about us?" Lucy flushed.

"He may be your brother, but he's also my best friend, you know."

"I suppose so," replied Lucy. "I mean, I've told quite a few people about you, too."

Scott raised his eyebrows in surprise.

Lucy flashed a wide smile at him. "So... okay."

"Okay?"

"We're a couple. Boyfriend and girlfriend. I guess Sayesha really is psychic."

"I already like her," Scott replied. "Now pull over,

miss," he said with mock authority. "We need to make this official."

Lucy checked the underside mirror and quickly dropped down to the ground-level breakdown lane. Scott reached for her, and this time, their embrace was not awkward at all. Lucy shivered a little as Scott's strong arms encircled her, and their lips met in a long, lingering caress.

"I've waited a long time for this," he said, breaking away to gaze at her. He gently stroked her hair.

"It's going to be a great summer," Lucy murmured in reply. "Even if we do have to deal with those terrible twins."

Chapter 3

"Are we there yet? Are we there yet? Are we there yet?"

The question was repeated rhythmically from behind Lucy—Romi's and Remi's voices in perfect unison. Lucy scrunched down in her seat, raised the shade on the plane window, and stuck her fingers in her ears. Despite her efforts to block out the noise, Romi's higher voice was still audible. "Are we there yet? Are we there..."

"Knock it off!" Lucy roared as she swiveled around in her seat. She glared at the boys. Remi seemed startled, but Romi stared right back at her, a sly smile on his lips.

"I've had it with the two of you! I'll bet everyone else on this plane feels the same way."

Lucy looked around and saw confirmation in the grim faces of nearby passengers.

"So sorry, cousin Lucy," Romi interjected. "We'll be sure not to bother the other passengers from now on."

"That's better."

Lucy settled back in her seat. Scott leaned in to whisper, "Good job. I knew you could keep those two in line."

A Doorway Through Time

"Are we there yet?" Thump... "Are we there yet?" Thump... "Are we there yet?" Thump...

The boys were now whispering their chant but accenting it with small kicks to the backs of Lucy's and Scott's seats. Lucy was about to turn around again when she heard Scott counting under his breath. When he got to ten, he gave Lucy a significant look. "I've got it this time."

He swiveled around until he had both boys in his sights. "If you don't cut it out right now, I'm going to..." he paused for emphasis, "take care of you when we get to Silvano."

Remi's eyes widened, but Romi appeared nonplussed. "Of course you will, 'cause you're going to be our babysitter. And we can't wait for you to take care of us," Romi replied, perfectly mimicking Scott's manner of speaking.

"I think you know what I mean."

"Oooh, I'm so scared. Aren't you, Remi?" Romi grinned and nudged his brother.

"Oh, yeah... I am!" Remi said in a quavering voice. He pretended to shiver.

Scott sighed. "What is it with you guys?"

As Romi and Remi looked at each other and giggled, Lucy felt a twinge...

I wonder if there's another telepath like Sayesha on this flight, she thought.

Romi turned back toward Scott. "We're just so young, and we have so much energy, and—well, there's simply nothing for us to do on this long, long flight." He sighed dramatically. "If only we had the money to download some new games, we'd be perfect angels, wouldn't we, Remi?"

Remi grinned up at Scott. "That's right, Captain Davenport, perfect angels."

"That's blackmail!" Lucy exclaimed, popping up over her seat.

"Oh my gosh. Did you know that?" Romi asked Remi in mock horror.

"Oh no," Remi answered in sickly sweet tones. "What were we thinking?"

Ellen, several rows ahead, finally noticed the conversation behind her. "Is everything okay back there?" she called.

"Everything's perfect, Aunt Ellen," Romi answered. He glanced at Remi, and they both sat placidly in their seats—models of good behavior.

Scott looked skeptically at the boys for a moment. "That's better," he finally mumbled.

Lucy, unconvinced, gave the boys a long, dirty look and settled back in her seat.

Silence reigned for the next few minutes. Scott took Lucy's hand and kissed her sweetly behind the ear. "We finally got them to settle down. We make a great team, Luce."

Loud kissing noises came from behind them. "Oh Scott, you're so hot," said Romi in a high-pitched voice.

"No, *you're* so hot," replied Remi in a slow, rumbling

impression of Scott.

Lucy shot Scott a look of horror.

"That's it," he growled, angling his large body around his seat to face the twins. "If I let you each download a game and charge it to my account, will you leave us alone and be quiet?"

"Sure—" Remi started to reply.

"Wait a minute," interrupted Romi. "Make that two games each, and you've got a deal." He looked defiantly at Scott. Remi, however, had the good sense to look nervously away.

"Fine," Scott replied. "You've won this time around. But believe me, this is the last time. I'm a lot bigger than you—and stronger. Accidents do happen, you know."

"Of course, Captain Davenport," said Romi. "We'll be good now."

The boys kept their part of the bargain and remained quiet for the remainder of the flight, but Ellen decided to separate the twins on the hoverbus ride, seating herself next to Romi and leaving Remi next to an elderly lady speaking Italian. Lucy gratefully enjoyed the view of fields and vineyards with Scott.

"Have you ever been to Europe?" Lucy asked.

"Never. And you?"

"No. I'd really like to visit some of the big cities on the weekends—Rome, Florence, Venice..."

"Absolutely," Scott agreed. After a pause, he asked, "So why exactly are we going to a town no one's ever heard of?"

"Silvano is supposed to be a beautiful little village, with lots of great hiking and astounding views. It should be really relaxing. And it's actually not that far from Rome—just kind of a slow trip around the mountains. Mom says the people there like to keep things the way they were in the old days. They have strict zoning laws for buildings and stuff, and Dr. Hartwick says they don't even have highways in Silvano—just one ground level lane for hovercars and buses."

Lucy looked around carefully, but since the chattering passengers were paying no attention to them, she leaned in to whisper, "Scott, the real reason we're going to Silvano is that it's a good central location for the international team Dr. Hartwick put together. He chose a spot out in the Italian countryside because no one would ever expect a group of scientists to be working on a top-secret project there. Anyone who knows they're in Italy thinks they're here for a team-building vacation. That's what we've told the twins and our neighbors back home. Oh, look—there's the villa!"

As the hoverbus rounded the bend, a valley appeared with narrow fields of grain rimmed by a train of golden hills. Low-slung cottages were clustered at the base of the largest hill. A steepled church with green-and-white striped marble walls dominated the village center. A winding road led up to a rambling mansion that hugged the craggy hillside. The setting sun gave the warmly colored stone walls an inviting glow.

"It's beautiful!" she exclaimed.

"Wow, it sure is," Scott agreed. "I've never stayed any place so fancy in my life."

The hoverbus let the small group off in front of the village church, where Ellen found a local resident with a battered hovercar who was willing to drive them up to the villa. As the car sputtered its way up the steep hill, Lucy scanned the villa grounds, hoping to catch a glimpse of Dr. Hartwick. At last, they pulled up outside the massive front doors, made of a dark wood intricately carved with geometric patterns. There was a loud creak as one of the doors slowly opened, and Lucy was delighted to see Dr. Hartwick appear. His face was creased in a wide grin, and his dark eyes twinkled. Lucy catapulted from the car and wrapped her arms around him in an enthusiastic embrace.

"Dr. Hartwick, it's so wonderful to see you!"

"Lucy, you haven't changed a bit! But could you please loosen your grip so I can breathe?"

Lucy laughed and stepped back. She looked at Dr. Hartwick critically. "You've changed. Your hair's more gray than black now."

It was Dr. Hartwick's turn to laugh as he ran his fingers through his tight curls.

29

"Tactful as ever, Lucy! I guess I can't stop time." He winked at her.

"But have you really figured out how to travel through time?" she whispered.

"Oh yes," he whispered back. There was a triumphant expression on his face.

"Can I see the... the you-know-what?"

"Talk to me after dinner," he murmured. He moved forward to greet the others.

Somehow, Lucy got through the long meal. She could hardly appreciate the fine pasta and steak they were served. She was too anxious to see the time machine for herself.

"I don't know why, but the food tastes different here," Scott remarked to Lucy.

Dr. Hartwick overheard the comment and leaned across the table to respond. "Scott, that's because in much of Europe—especially in rural areas—people have resisted many of the modern amenities we take for granted at home. This is a perfect example. Italians have always taken great pride in their cooking, and many people refuse to use carbon replicators to create their food. So everything you've eaten is from locally raised animals and locally grown produce."

"No wonder," said Lucy. "Donald would have really loved this."

"We'll have to tell him about it," Scott replied. "Maybe

it will help convince him to join us for a weekend."

Lucy tried to keep her mind off the time machine by chatting with Scott and the scientists seated near her. To her great relief, Dr. Hartwick finally pushed his chair away from the table and patted his ample belly. "It has been delightful to share this fine dinner and catch up with all of you," he smiled at Ellen, Lucy, and Scott, "and to meet you fine young men," he turned to the twins, who had been uncharacteristically quiet. "However, I have a few things I really need to finish up in the lab. If you will forgive me, I'd like to attend to that before I join you—perhaps for a game of cards or a movie?" He looked inquisitively at Ellen.

"I know how you feel about your work, Roland, and you won't really be able to relax until you feel you have things in order. Don't worry about me. I'm pretty jet-lagged from the flight. I wouldn't mind turning in early." She eyed the twins, who were starting to nod off in their seats. "I think my nephews would agree with me."

"Well then, good night all," replied Dr. Hartwick. He paused to look Lucy directly in the eye and pressed a note into her hand before he exited the dining room.

"Huh? What?" said Romi, suddenly aware of the movement about him. He poked Remi, who was beginning to snore.

"Bedtime," said Ellen as she stood up and pulled the boys—resisting—from their chairs. "Good night all," she said before heading out the door with the twins in tow.

Scott was talking with an elderly scientist from England, and Lucy waited impatiently for a lull in the conversation.

What on Earth is so interesting about fluid mechanics? she wondered.

Finally she could wait no longer and interrupted Scott mid-sentence. "I'd like to get unpacked and settled in. Wouldn't you, Scott?"

"No, I think I'll hang out here a little longer," he replied without glancing her way.

Lucy cleared her throat and Scott finally turned his head. Seeing the stormy look in her eyes, he quickly back-tracked. "Actually Lucy, that's probably a good idea. I guess I'll get settled, too. Uh, good night, Dr. Emerson."

They quietly left the room together, but as soon as they were out of earshot, Scott turned to Lucy in frustration. "What was that all about? Why did you want me to leave?"

She unfolded the note. "Dr. Hartwick is going to show us the time machine. But nobody can know!"

"Excellent!" Scott's bad mood instantly dissipated. "Let's go!"

Chapter 4

∿ ∿ ∿

They raced down the long corridor, their feet echoing on the marble floors. At last they reached the lab. Lucy rapped quietly on the thick, wooden door. Dr. Hartwick answered her knock, carefully opening the door before stopping in consternation. "Scott, too?"

"Oh puh-lease, Dr. Hartwick. After all we've been through together?"

His face softened. "Yes... yes, of course. I was just surprised." He poked his head out of the doorway and looked up and down the hall. "Good, it's clear. Quickly!"

The lab was very large and medieval-looking, like every room in the villa. It had checkerboard black-and-white marble floors, and stone walls with fluted arches supporting the high-beamed ceiling. Banks of computers, humming in the relative quiet, seemed the only concession to the 21st century. Lucy looked around in surprise.

"I thought... but where is it?"

"My dear, we could not keep a valuable piece of equipment in a room where anybody could have access to it. A little security is required, I'm sure you'll agree. Follow me."

Dr. Hartwick led them to a narrow door set in a far corner of the room. He opened it with a flourish. "Here we are!"

"But Dr. Hartwick, that's a broom closet!" Scott objected.

"It looks like a broom closet. But appearances are deceiving. Behold."

Dr. Hartwick reached behind the doorframe and pushed a small button. The mop, broom and cleaning products shimmered for a moment, then disappeared. In their place was a shining metal door with a black rectangle in the center.

"All the stuff we saw was a hologram?" guessed Scott.

"Yes, indeed," replied Dr. Hartwick. "Pretty good, don't you think?"

"It completely fooled me," answered Lucy. "But Dr. Hartwick, the door it was hiding has no handle or doorknob. How do you get in?"

"This door is actually a sort of security gate," explained Dr. Hartwick.

He pressed his right hand firmly on the black rectangle. A band of red light pulsed from the top and moved vertically. When the light reached the bottom, the door slid aside with a hiss, revealing an open elevator.

"At the moment, I am the only one authorized to open

the gate after hours, although your mother's data will be entered in the morning," Dr. Hartwick said to Lucy as they stepped into the small white cubicle.

Lucy looked around apprehensively. "If this is an elevator, Dr. Hartwick, do you think I could take the stairs?"

"I know you get claustrophobic, Lucy, but believe me—this is better than the alternative. We're going to be going down the equivalent of 12 stories below ground."

Lucy gulped. "Shut in a small space, going deep underground. Perfect."

Scott put a reassuring arm around her. "It'll be over in no time. And just think of the payback."

"Believe me, that's what I'm focusing on," muttered Lucy as the door closed. "Hey—why aren't there any buttons?"

"They are unnecessary. This is a one-stop elevator. If you get on in the villa, you are going subterranean. If you get on in the cave, you must want to return above ground."

"That does make sense," Lucy grudgingly agreed. She gave a little shiver and leaned in closer to Scott.

"Try saying the alphabet backwards in your head," suggested Scott. "It helps me when I'm nervous."

"If you say so," Lucy agreed again, but gave it a try. *Whoa, it's harder than I thought,* she realized with surprise.

She had only managed to go haltingly from 'Z' to 'M' when there was a small lurch, and the elevator door opened silently.

"This is incredible!" Scott exclaimed.

Lucy quickly stepped out and paused in amazement.

"It looks like a stadium dome," she said breathlessly. "Only no Astroturf on the ground."

The elevator had opened into an enormous space, entirely encased in gleaming metal. In the center of the room rose a tall, slender metal column. Connected perpendicularly to it was a dull grey, capsule-shaped pod, about the size of a large hovercar. The column and pod were encased within a larger, glass-like tube. The clear tube was embedded with a lacework of wires, and pocked with metallic circles at regular intervals. The whole system was mounted on a circular, black base.

Dr. Hartwick was beaming with pleasure. "The machine is quite a sight, isn't it?"

"That's a time machine?" Lucy blurted out. "I thought it was some kind of underground utility pole."

"I suppose it doesn't look like much on the outside," said Dr. Hartwick stiffly. "But what happens inside is nothing short of a miracle."

Oops, thought Lucy.

"I'm sure it's so elegantly designed it looks simple," Scott agreed quickly. "Right, Lucy?" he asked pointedly.

"Oh, right. Sorry, Dr. Hartwick. Can you show us how it works?"

"Well... ah..."

"Can you *explain* how it works?" Scott asked.

A Doorway Through Time

Dr. Hartwick rubbed his hands together in anticipation. "First, I'll address Scott's question about time travel. Ready for a little physics?"

"My favorite subject," returned Lucy with a smile.

Scott raised one eyebrow in surprise.

"No, really," she insisted.

"Come, let's sit down. Perfect! We're going to go way back," began Dr. Hartwick. "Back to the early 20th century, to Dr. Albert Einstein and his General Theory of Relativity. According to this theory, space and time are linked, creating what we call spacetime. We know it to be more than a theory, because the three of us experienced an actual anomaly in spacetime when we traveled across the galaxy. The stable wormhole we discovered was the result of a warping in the fabric of space. Remember, too, that while only a few days had passed for us on Earth, many months had passed in the same time interval for the crew of the *Argonaut*. The differences in time were further evidence of that twisted space and time connection. So far, so good?"

"Sure," Lucy agreed as Scott soberly nodded.

"So let's think about that wormhole. The wormhole formed as a result of an incredible chain of events: first, a nuclear explosion in space caused the massive expansion of a naturally occurring, subatomic wormhole. Then, the wormhole remained open because its 'mouth' expanded in a loop of cosmic string. It would be nearly impossible to replicate that chain of events. So I was forced to think of other ways to reliably warp time and space."

Dr. Hartwick put his arms around Lucy and Scott and whispered conspiratorially. "Guess what? We experience real warping of spacetime every day. Do you know how?"

Lucy shook her head.

"It keeps us anchored to the ground." Dr. Hartwick hinted.

"Gravity?" asked Scott in amazement.

"The very same. There is no gravity in open space. That's because gravity is connected to mass. Massive objects, like stars and planets—and especially black holes— actually warp the fabric of spacetime. We can't see, touch or feel this warping. But we can experience its side effect, which is gravity. The more massive the object, the more powerful its gravitational pull. That's why we can jump higher on the moon than on Earth. The Earth is more massive than the moon, so Earth's gravity is stronger."

"This is all very interesting, Dr. Hartwick," interrupted Lucy, "but I don't see what it has to do with that thing in the middle of the cave."

"Patience is a virtue, my dear Lucy," responded Dr. Hartwick with a small smile, "which, along with tact, are traits you have never possessed in abundance."

"Nailed!" said Scott with a grin.

Ouch, thought Lucy.

"Now, you know that cardinal law of physics, that for every action, there is an equal but opposite reaction?"

continued Dr. Hartwick.

"Yes, since third grade," Lucy said impatiently.

"I've told you that gravity is an aftereffect of space-time warping. But gravity itself can curve space. If you could generate enough gravity in a lab, you could theoretically twist time into a loop, or what some scientists refer to as a 'closed time-like curve.' You could jump into that loop at one point in spacetime, and jump out again into another point in spacetime—perhaps to go on a dinosaur safari. Time travel!"

"But how did you create the gravity required? Did you make a black hole?" asked Scott in an awed voice.

Dr. Hartwick looked abashed. "That's a very good guess, and I wish that were the case. But no, our technology is not there yet. I succeeded in another way. I adapted the work of a professor from the University of Connecticut, Roland Mallett, who also looked back to Dr. Einstein. According to Einstein's Theory of General Relativity, matter is not the only thing that can create a gravitational field. Light can, too. So if gravity can affect time... and light can create gravity... then light can affect time."

"So your time travel machine is powered by light?" ventured Lucy.

"Not powered by light, but it does use light to create time loops. Decades ago, Dr. Mallett created a time machine of sorts by building a unidirectional ring laser. The circulating light stirred up the space inside a small column,

Judith Bourassa Joy

creating a closed time loop capable of sending a subatomic particle forward in time."

"If Dr. Mallett managed to do this a long time ago, why doesn't every country have a time machine now?"

"Once again, theory has been limited by reality. There were two big problems. Number one: we have never before possessed an energy source capable of sustaining the light needed to create a time loop traversable by humans. Number two is a well-known constraint: you can't travel back to a time before the time machine was turned on. It creates an impossible situation. You could create a time machine, wait a year, and then travel back in time to a year earlier, when the machine was created. But no further. Do you see what I mean?"

"Whoa, that's kind of hard to take in," said Scott.

"That's really disappointing," said Lucy in a strained voice.

"Have faith!" exclaimed Dr. Hartwick. "Lucy's parents solved problem number one, and I solved problem number two."

"My parents?" asked Lucy in wonder.

"Let me start with my own contribution first," said Dr. Hartwick. "I realized that although you can't travel back in a time machine to a time before its invention, you don't really need to. My time machine creates a time loop that can go back millions of years. Once the time loop is created, it's like an ocean current: you sit in a sort of 'boat,' slip into the time current, and let the current take you to a specific point in time. Then, you maneuver your 'boat' out of the current. When you want to go home, you get back in your vessel and slip back into the current. Because it is a time loop, it will always take you back to your starting point. The time machine itself never left. You just took a ride in the time loop it created."

"Brilliant!" exclaimed Scott.

"That's amazing, Dr. Hartwick. But how about the problem that my parents solved?" asked Lucy.

"In a word, antimatter."

"What?" asked Scott, bewildered.

"Every force has its opposite, correct?"

"Yes," replied Scott.

"We are all made of mass, or matter. Everything you can touch is matter. But there is an opposite to that—antimatter. You can't touch it or see it, but it's there, all around us. The trick is to safely manufacture significant quantities of it for human use. Most scientists think that's mere science fiction. But Lucy's parents were—are—hardly ordinary scientists."

He pointed to a pipe, running along the perimeter of the room about 10 feet above the floor.

"Do you see that pipe? It's a new kind of particle accelerator that we use to create subatomic collisions yielding large amounts of antimatter. The antimatter is fed through underground tubes into the black base of the time machine, where it powers the lights used to create and maintain time loops. The machine must stay on for the whole time that a traveler needs the loop. That takes a tremendous amount of energy. More than anyone has been able to manufacture before."

"And is antimatter really that powerful?" Lucy wondered aloud.

"Oh, yes. Antimatter is the most awesome source of power ever identified in the universe. A gram of antimatter—about the weight of a penny—is enough to power a mid-sized city for a month. Put another way, it's a thousand times more powerful than a nuclear warhead. We treat it very, very carefully."

Dr. Hartwick spread his arms wide and slowly rotated in place. "The metal coating this room is no ordinary steel. It is a special metal alloy, made from elements we discovered on Mars. In theory, it should contain the effects of an antimatter blast in the event of an accident. Of course, any person caught in this room would be instantly incinerated."

Scott looked around the cavern nervously. Lucy simply shrugged.

"Looks pretty safe now," she said with a grin. "So walk us through the time machine, Dr. Hartwick. How do the pieces work?"

"Well, the walls of the clear, polycarbonate column contain banks of high-powered gamma ray lasers. The lasers' light penetrates the space inside the silver column, creating a gravitational force that effectively swirls up space and causes that closed time loop I described. I can adjust the angle of the lasers so that your trip begins either backward or forward in time. When the lasers are set to minimum power, a time loop of about a year is possible. Set them at maximum power, and I believe a time loop of several million years is achievable."

Lucy's heart was pounding. "Please, show us," she pleaded.

Dr. Hartwick looked suddenly worried. "You understand that you must never breathe a word of this to anyone! There are many individuals and governments who would love to get their hands on this. We would all be in grave danger if news got out."

"We understand, sir," said Scott in a strong, reassuring voice.

"Of course, Dr. Hartwick," agreed Lucy.

"I know you'll be discreet, but there have been some disturbing threats recently... But never mind, I've just been on edge lately," Dr. Hartwick blustered.

Lucy and Scott exchanged worried glances.

"Pay no attention to me. Come along."

As they drew near the time machine, Lucy could better appreciate its massive size. They entered through a door in the base. From there, they had to climb a small ladder to a trap door that opened into the transparent column.

Dr. Hartwick approached the silver capsule and gave

it a fond pat. "You travel in the pod, here," he explained. "If the wormhole we used to travel across the galaxy was a kind of doorway through space, then this, my friends, is a kind of doorway through time."

They opened the capsule door and entered a window-less, compact vehicle with a bank of controls at one end. Two rows of two seats were behind the controls. A wall rose behind the seats, with a slim pair of doors.

"What's behind the doors?" Lucy wondered.

"Storage," Dr. Hartwick answered. "Now take a look at these controls. We had a human interface designer make them very easy to use."

He sat down in one of the captain's chairs and pressed a button marked Power. Instantly, the pod's control panel lit up. Next to the power button was a sliderbar marked Laser Intensity.

"This vessel is essentially a big remote control. It has a small engine, just enough to start up the time machine and push the pod into, or out of, the time loop in the col-umn. Now watch this," Dr. Hartwick beamed. "As I push the sliderbar to the right, the laser intensity that's required increases. The display next to my slider changes to reflect the size of my time loop."

Lucy and Scott looked in awe as the monitor's display showed an image of a glowing loop that changed in rela-tion to the slider's movement, expanding as Dr. Hartwick moved it from one year, to one decade, to one century, to one millennium.

"If you have a specific date in mind, you can even do a manual override," Dr. Hartwick explained, pointing to a keypad below the slider marked Manual Entry. "Let me show you that. What date do you want?"

"The day I was born?" ventured Lucy.

Dr. Hartwick looked apologetically at Lucy. "I remember it's coming up soon, but I don't recall exactly when.

"July 17, 2048," she replied.

Dr. Hartwick sat down in the pilot's seat and pushed the numbers on the keypad in rapid succession, so that the number 07.17.2048 appeared on the monitor. "Of course, that could be either AD on the timescale or BC for my paleontologist friends, so we have to tell the machine which period it is."

He pushed a toggle button for AD, which then appeared at the end of the date. Then he pressed Enter. Lucy watched closely as the picture of the time loop shrank and a new screen came to life, displaying a progress bar and the word Calibrating. After a few seconds, another button lit up, marked Activate.

"And this is where we stop," Dr. Hartwick said with finality. He swiveled around to look squarely at Lucy and Scott. "Pressing the Activate button would automatically trigger the flow of antimatter into the time machine's engine, located in the black base below this pod. The antimatter pools up in the containment chamber to provide the intense power needed to spark the process. It would be very dangerous to stop the machine at that point, so the controls won't even allow it."

"Then you'd better hope you entered your date right," said Lucy with a nervous laugh.

"You don't hope. You know," replied Dr. Hartwick. "You act slowly and carefully—and double-check your work."

Lucy flushed and nodded. Scott reached for her hand and squeezed it sympathetically.

Dr. Hartwick turned back toward the controls. "Supposing I had pressed Activate, a circular hatch in the metal column of the machine would open up once the time loop was ready. Then the pod's engine would propel it into the time loop, inside the column."

"And we would pop back in time to see me as a baby," concluded Lucy.

"After we hiked out of the cavern, found transportation to the nearest airport, flew to Boston, and drove to the hospital," answered Dr. Hartwick with a smile.

"What do you mean?" asked Lucy. "Why don't we just appear outside the hospital?"

"What you have to understand, Lucy, is that you would travel back to July 17, 2048, here in this cavern," explained Dr. Hartwick.

"Oh—" broke in Scott, in sudden understanding. "The time machine moves you in time, but not in place."

A Doorway Through Time

"Exactly," nodded Dr. Hartwick. "You will always travel to a different point in time, but arriving here in this cavern. We have a long list of researchers with their own particular interests in the history of the Italian peninsula. Each research team has created historically accurate clothing and equipment that will enable them to blend in with the natives at the points in time they want to visit. There's even gear for prehistoric research, as I know of at least one group that wants to study the local Jurassic-era dinosaurs. The costumes and equipment are all ready and waiting in the cabinet at the back."

"So you're ready to start sending scientists back in time?" Scott asked.

"Yes, the first trial is scheduled for two weeks from tomorrow. Assuming the latest threat is..." Dr. Hartwick's voice trailed off. He gave himself a little shake and forced a smile. "Yes, the Tuesday after next, I believe."

"This is a lot to take in," Lucy gasped. "What you've done is incredibly impressive, Dr. Hartwick, but this small space is getting to me. I feel like I need to get above ground now. Is that okay with you, Scott?"

"Of course," answered Scott.

"Time to say good-bye to the time machine," said Dr. Hartwick as he pushed the power button off.

"For now," murmured Lucy.

Chapter 5

Lucy and Scott were not invited to the secret laboratory again. Instead, they spent their days trailing after the twins, who seemed content to explore the fields and forested hills. Lucy and Scott enjoyed the outdoor activity, and were grateful that the boys were busily engaged. In the evenings, they all watched movies or played games, and Lucy began an electronic pen-pal correspondence with Sayesha. After nearly a week of this, however, Lucy was ready for a change.

"What would you think about taking the boys to Rome?" Lucy suggested to Scott one morning.

Scott's face lit up. "That would be awesome! This is a beautiful valley, but I'd love to see the city."

"All right, then! You go tell the twins, and I'll grab my guidebook to Rome."

"Let's hope the boys are into Roman history," Scott said to her retreating back.

To Scott and Lucy's amazement, however, Romi and Remi were very excited about the trip. They talked non-stop on the slow hoverbus ride, giving Lucy and Scott a mini-lecture on the major milestones of the Roman empire. Lucy listened as she paged through her guidebook, and finally interrupted Romi as he was wrapping up a story about the fall of Rome.

"The Roman Forum," she said, tapping her finger on the screen of her e-reader. "That's what I want to see most. Can you help us figure out what we're looking at?"

"Of course!" exclaimed Remi in disbelief. "Mom has taught us all about the buildings that used to be there."

"You would be the experts," Scott said. The boys looked suspiciously at him, trying to discern if he was being sarcastic or not, but only Lucy saw Scott give her a quick wink.

Romi and Remi proved to be impressively knowledgeable. Lucy was taken aback by the sheer size and crumbling magnificence of the ancient forum. The narrow roads were still visible, as were many of the pavers, in what was once a giant, open-air market. Columns rose jaggedly from the bases of broken buildings, and Lucy strained to imagine how the forum's markets and temples looked in their prime. She studied the nearest set of ruins, trying unsuccessfully to match it to the descriptions in her guidebook.

"I think that's the Basilica Julia," she ventured, "built during Julius Caesar's time."

"No, no!" Romi said impatiently. "That's way down

the road, on the other side of the Sacra Via."

Lucy's blank face registered her lack of comprehension.

"You know, the Sacred Road—the one we're walking on right now?"

Romi's loud, slow tone made it clear that he doubted Lucy's mental abilities, and she flushed with annoyance. Before she could respond, Remi put a soft hand on her arm. "You're looking at the Basilica of Maxentius," he said. "It was built way after Julius Caesar's time, during the Christian era. See, here it is in your book."

Remi became their official tour guide after that, while Romi explored ahead of the other three. They clambered over the remains of more basilicas and so many temples that Lucy could hardly keep their names straight. As they rounded the corner of the Basilica Aemilia, they came upon Romi staring up at a statue of a female wolf. Two infants were carved below her, drinking from the wolf's engorged teats.

"What the…?" Scott began.

"Romulus and Remus," Remi answered. "They were abandoned by their parents—" He paused and gave Romi a significant look— "and were raised by wolves. Years later, they came out of the wilderness and founded Rome on the seven hills."

"Pretty weird myth," Lucy commented.

"It's not a myth," Romi snapped. "It's the truth. You should take a picture, Lucy."

A Doorway Through Time

"Whatever," Lucy reluctantly agreed. *It's a pretty freaky statue, but I guess it's worth it if it shuts him up*, she thought. She used her contacts to take a couple of photos, ignoring Romi's angry glances.

Finally, the twins let them move on, and they continued their rambling explorations. As the sun began to set on the Palatine hill, which Remi explained was the home of the Roman kings, Scott glanced down at his watch. "It's been great having you take us around, Remi, but the bus will be leaving pretty soon. We'd better find Romi and get out of here."

The boys were quiet on the way home, giving Lucy a chance to send a message to Sayesha, describing the sights of the day.

The truce between the twins and their babysitters was short-lived, however. The very next day, Romi and Remi began bickering with one another and teasing Scott and Lucy again. In desperation, Lucy loaned them her hoverboard, and they spent an afternoon trying out flips and tricks. After a couple of hours of this, however, there was a loud crack and a yell. Lucy ran outside and discovered her hoverboard, split and splintered, on the ground. Remi lay nearby, rubbing his head and howling.

"You little—" Lucy began, racing toward them in both fear and rage.

Just then, Ellen rushed outside, having overheard the noise. "Now, Lucy, hoverboards can be replaced," she chided. "Skulls can't. Are you okay, Remi?"

Remi stopped crying and shook his head.

Lucy took a deep breath and shouted as she turned back toward the villa, "It took me a whole year to save enough money for that hoverboard!"

From the corner of her eye, she saw Romi laughing openly at her.

I'll get you somehow, she thought in fury.

You just try, she heard a voice in her head say.

Surprised, Lucy whirled on her heel to glare at Romi, but he quickly assumed an innocent face and moved toward his brother in seeming concern.

Lucy closed her mind and stormed inside, seething.

The next day, the boys declared they were tired of wandering outdoors and wanted to explore the villa instead. The villa's sprawling layout and hidden passageways made it impossible for Lucy and Scott to keep an eye on the boys. They suspected that Romi and Remi really planned to torment the villa's residents, but it was difficult to prove the twins' intent.

Scott woke with a yell one night, slapping frantically at biting red ants that swarmed over him. Further investigation revealed crumbled biscotti at the bottom of his sheets, apparently left to attract the stinging insects. And over a short period of time, Dr. Hartwick's belongings were constantly being misplaced, which he first blamed on his own absent-mindedness. As the days went on, however, his slippers turned up in the freezer, while a scholarly article he was writing was discovered in the flour bin. Even he grew suspicious. The last straw came almost two weeks into their stay. Romi and Remi had been busy outside in the fields all day, and Lucy and Scott were too glad of the respite to investigate. Lucy was sketching the Italian landscape while Scott read *A Room with a View* aloud to her. The spreading branches of an olive tree protected them from the sun, but Lucy still had to squint to make out the angle of the hills in the distance, distorted somewhat by heat waves that shimmered in the strong light. Without warning, hysterical screams broke the idyllic moment. "Oh, il mio Dio! Uscire! Uscire! Lei i topi escono dalla mia cucina!"

"It's Renata, the cook," Lucy announced with sudden understanding. "She's yelling at someone to get out of her kitchen. Someone must have broken into the villa!"

Scott threw down his book, and he and Lucy raced back to the villa. As they approached the side door, they saw Romi and Remi in a shaded corner of the courtyard, doubled up in mirth.

"This can't be good," Scott muttered as they headed toward the kitchen.

Utter chaos met them. Renata was running about the kitchen, swatting the floor with an old willow broom. At least two dozen mice scurried about in frantic confusion, trying to dodge Renata's blows. Lucy grabbed a mop and

53

Judith Bourassa Joy

Scott found another broom, and they set about herding the mice toward the back door. After half an hour of concerted effort, the mice were gone. Renata turned to Lucy and held her arm firmly. She leaned in, forcing Lucy to look straight into her eyes. "Those mice, it was no accident they come into my cucina—how you say, my kitchen. Your cousins, they are the devil!" Renata briefly closed her eyes and crossed herself. "Never am I working here again—not while they are here!"

"Renata please," Lucy begged, "Scott and I will keep a better eye on the boys."

"No! I never come back until those two are gone!"

Lucy and Scott were unable to dissuade her, and they watched in dismay as Renata stumped off down the road to her cottage.

"Mom is going to kill us," Lucy moaned.

"I'm going to kill the boys," replied Scott.

The twins, predictably, were nowhere to be found, and Lucy and Scott had to break the news to Ellen and Dr. Hartwick. They headed for the research lab, and Lucy cautiously opened the door. The scientists were busy finishing up their work for the day. "Uh, Mom, Dr. Hartwick—could we talk to you for a second?" Lucy asked.

Ellen looked up with a smile, which quickly faded when she saw the expression on Lucy's face. She nudged Dr. Hartwick, and they hurriedly stepped into the hall. Ellen carefully closed the lab door and turned ominously toward Lucy. "What's wrong?"

Lucy and Scott took turns describing the fracas in the kitchen. When they finished, Dr. Hartwick, usually imperturbable, flushed a deep red under his dark skin. "Lucy, how could you let this happen? We're doing very important work here, and the team cannot afford any setbacks!"

Much to Lucy's surprise, Ellen showed no anger, just a kind of regret. "I'm afraid I'm really the one to blame, Roland. I never should have given in to Rhea and taken the boys. I didn't realize just how bad they would be." She gave Lucy and Scott a wan smile. "It's not your fault. I know you did the best you could."

Ellen's unexpected sympathy made Lucy feel far worse than anger would have. Before she could think of how to respond, however, Ellen continued, "I suppose we'd better find the boys now."

While the other scientists left for the village restaurant, Dr. Hartwick, Ellen, Lucy and Scott fruitlessly searched the grounds of the villa. After a hasty, cold supper, they decided to check again inside the villa. Scott finally discovered Koml and Reml in their own beds, asleep. Their faces, surrounded by soft, dark curls, were cherubic in the moonlight. *How can two boys who act like devils look like angels?* wondered Lucy.

"I can't decide whether to wake them up and teach them a lesson, or leave them alone and enjoy a night without them," Scott muttered.

"An evening without them seems too good to give up," whispered Ellen. "Let's deal with them in the morning. I'll try to speak with Rhea tonight about sending them to her in Indonesia. I hate to give up, but these boys are just way too out of control."

Ellen headed toward her own bedroom while Lucy and Scott walked back to the sitting room in silence. Scott finally broke the glum atmosphere. "Want to take a walk, Lucy?"

"I think I need a little time alone, Scott," Lucy said in a strained voice.

He nodded in understanding. "Okay, see you in the morning."

They kissed goodnight, and Lucy crept out the side door of the villa into the soft blackness of evening. Nearby crickets abruptly halted their grating song, while their distant neighbors enthusiastically continued their discordant chorus. Lucy leaned against the stone wall of the building, grateful for its smooth coldness and for the light breeze that was beginning to dissipate the heat of another midsummer day. She looked up, automatically scanning the sky for familiar stars. A sudden pressure in her head alerted her to tense emotions in the villa, and she strained to overhear voices speaking nearby.

"I just got another alert from the agency in D.C. This is the third threat to our facility in the past month, Ellen," Dr. Hartwick was saying in anxious tones. "Somehow, news of our work has been leaked, and at least two foreign governments are determined to gain control of our machine."

"So we need to step up our security, Roland," replied Ellen soothingly. "Our first trial is only two days away! Just hire more guards and beef up our security system."

"If a powerful nation with a top-class spy network sets its mind to it, there's no way we can protect the time machine. Ellen, think about it! Can you imagine what kind of damage an unfriendly nation could cause by using the time machine to change its own history? We could wake up and find that the world is a totally different place. Maybe we'd find that Hitler had won World War II the second time around! If this machine or its specifications fall into the wrong hands, it could be disastrous!"

Lucy tiptoed alongside the wall of the villa until she stood next to her mother's bedroom window. She peeped in and saw Dr. Hartwick pacing about the room. Lucy's mother was seated in a corner of the room, gripping the arms of her chair so that her knuckles were white. Ellen's voice was steely. "Surely, this isn't the first time these concerns have occurred to you."

"No. But I have to admit, I really didn't think we would succeed."

Lucy heard her mother gasp.

"Let me amend that. For once in my life, I had ample funding to do the kind of pure research that I love best. I thought we would make some important discoveries and add to our understanding of quantum physics. I was not convinced that we could create a machine capable of taking us into the past and future. And now... here we are on the brink of success, with an actual time machine ready to test."

"And what better use of it than to go back to April 2064 and try to save my—to save the crew of the *Icarus*?" Ellen's voice had a pleading note to it now.

Lucy saw Dr. Hartwick go over to her mother and kneel down by her side. He gently placed his hand over hers. "Ellen, dear... you must see that we have created our own Frankenstein." He paused and took a deep breath. "And now we must destroy it."

Ellen shook off his hands and pushed him aside as she exploded in anger. "You just don't want to save Henry. You want me for yourself, but I don't feel the same way about you. You don't care about protecting the world. You're just selfish!"

Lucy watched in shock as tears began streaming down her usually stoic mother's face.

Ellen ran from the room, leaving Dr. Hartwick alone in his stunned disbelief. Lucy flattened herself against the villa wall trying to comprehend what she had just overheard. Her head was pounding from the onslaught of emotions. Dazed, she was able to formulate just one thought. *I've got to talk to Scott.*

Chapter 6

Scott stroked his chin with his thumb as he considered what Lucy had told him. "I never noticed Dr. Hartwick had a thing for your mom. Did you?"

"Kind of. I mean, I could sense strong emotions from him every time he was near Mom, but I tried not to think about it. I didn't want to believe it," Lucy admitted. "And now he wants to destroy the time machine. So they won't be able to save my dad! It makes me so angry!"

Scott looked at Lucy in genuine surprise. "Is that what it's all about for you? Because I thought the goal of this machine was to let us observe Earth's history firsthand— whether it was dinosaurs roaming Pangea, Julius Caesar building his empire, or Michelangelo painting the Sistine Chapel."

"Of course that's what it's really supposed to be about!" Lucy cried in exasperation. "But why shouldn't my father be saved? He's an important part of my history!"

"Lucy, if we take that attitude, then everyone on Earth is going to want to use the time machine to save the lives of their own loved ones. And in doing so, they may change history in a way that hurts other people. The time machine can't be used for personal reasons."

"Fine, then it should just be used one time for one very personal reason. The crew of the *Icarus* was martyred for the International Space Agency. And that same agency built the time machine and is going to reap astronomical sums of money from it. They owe it to my father to save his life now!"

Lucy crossed her arms and looked defiantly at Scott. His eyes narrowed as he regarded her suspiciously. "I don't need to be a mind reader to know what you're planning, Lucy. You're going to use the time machine. I don't suppose there's anything I can say to stop you?"

"Nothing at all. I know that if our roles were reversed, my dad would do the same for me. The question is... are you coming with me?"

Lucy waited in silence as Scott considered the situation. Finally he spoke. "I know what you're capable of, Lucy. I doubt that anyone could stop you, short of shackling you in prison—and even then, I bet you'd find a way out." He paused for a moment, then continued, "I don't feel right letting you do this alone, so... I'm coming along for the ride. Again." He smiled ruefully.

Lucy's frosty demeanor melted at his sympathetic response. "But Scott, you're likely to get kicked out of school—or worse. You're technically an adult, and I'm technically not."

"And that's a technicality I'm not going to worry about," he replied. He stepped closer and gathered Lucy into his arms. "You took me on a great adventure once before. And this is your dad we're talking about." He gave her a wicked grin. "I suppose now I'll get to ask him for permission to date you!"

Lucy rolled her eyes. "Yeah, right. But first we have to figure out how to break into the lab. Only my mom and Dr. Hartwick have security clearance to open the doors after hours. And we need to work fast. I wouldn't put it past Dr. Hartwick to destroy that thing tomorrow morning."

They discussed various strategies for over an hour, but could not come up with a plausible plan.

"If only we had some explosives to break open the door," Scott grumbled in exasperation. "Or if only the room were locked with an old-fashioned key. The fingerprint scanner is foolproof!"

He picked up a chunk of clay the twins had been sculpting with earlier in the day and began rolling it between his fingers.

Lucy watched disinterestedly as she continued inventing, and rejecting, plans in her head. Scott flattened the clay in his hands and pressed it down on a nearby table. Lucy sat up with a start.

"That's it!" she crowed in triumph.

"What's it?"

"Look at the clay!"

Scott looked at the flat piece of clay, its smooth surface marred only by the light marks his fingertips had left behind.

"I don't get it," he said.

"Scott, we can make an impression of my mom's hand in the clay while she sleeps. She's a deep sleeper. Then we can make a cast of it and fool the scanner!"

"I don't know, but let's try it," he agreed.

Lucy and Scott scraped up all the clay they could find, and Lucy kneaded it into a warm, flat pancake.

"I'll take the impression," Lucy told Scott. "If my mom does wake up, it will seem less weird if I'm the one in her room. You can hunt for something made of rubber that we can melt."

"I'm on it. Meet you back here in 15 minutes."

A quarter of an hour later, Lucy returned triumphantly to Scott's bedroom. He was seated next to a small, portable oven, holding a large bowl.

"I did my part," exulted Lucy. "How about you?"

"I got the stove from the pantry and broke into the villa's first aid kits to collect the latex gloves. I think they'll work." He tipped the bowl to display his cache. "Now let's bake your clay for a few minutes before we melt up this stuff."

Half an hour later, the clay was hard and cool, and the gloves had melted into a cloudy, sticky liquid. Lucy stood by the window watching as Scott, hardly breathing because of the fumes, tipped the mess of latex into the clay cast. He quickly put the cast into his mini-refrigerator and joined her by the window. They leaned their heads outside and breathed in the fresh air.

"Ten minutes?" Scott asked.

"Sounds good," Lucy replied.

Ten minutes later, Lucy took their experiment from the refrigerator and cautiously tugged at the rubber. Nothing happened. She pulled harder, and the latex reluctantly separated from the clay. Lucy held up her prize in delight. "It's a perfect impression of Mom's hand! You can see all the lines on her fingers!"

"Awesome!" exclaimed Scott. "Now let's see if we can fool the scanner."

They tiptoed down the corridor, passing the rooms of the scientific staff. It was nearly midnight, and they were reassured by the sounds of snores emanating from the rooms in a variety of octaves. "Apparently, snoring is a job prerequisite," whispered Scott.

Lucy stifled a giggle. She became sober, however, as they approached the lab door. The room's motion sensor automatically switched on the lights as they entered. Lucy quickly found a manual switch and turned them off.

"I hope nobody noticed the lights," said Scott in a worried tone.

"Too late now. Let's move fast," Lucy replied tersely.

Judith Bourassa Joy

She switched on her flashlight, and they headed for the elevator entrance. Lucy turned off the hologram display, and the security gate came into view. She carefully held the latex impression to the scanner surface. There was a loud beep, and a message lit up the screen in red letters: IN-VALID. "What do we do now?" asked Lucy in despair.

"Let me try," answered Scott. "Maybe it's got a heat sensor, too." He took the impression and held it between his hands for a few minutes. "Now it's close to the temperature of my hands," he murmured.

Scott pressed the impression firmly against the glass panel of the scanner. Lucy held her breath as a line of red light moved vertically down the panel, checking every millimeter of the impression. Once the light reached the bottom of the panel, the gate slid open. "You did it!" Lucy exclaimed, throwing her arms around Scott. "We are the best team!"

They allowed themselves a long, luxurious kiss as the elevator traveled down. "For luck," whispered Scott with a smile as they stepped out of the elevator and into the cavern. The lights automatically turned on.

"I guess we don't need to worry about these lights," said Lucy with a nervous laugh.

"No, we've got bigger worries," Scott answered as he started toward the time machine.

"Wait a minute, Scott. I want to leave a note. When I go out at home, I always let Mom know where I'll be. I think... I'd like to do that now. So she and Dr. Hartwick know why we're doing this."

"That's a great idea. I would never blaze my own trail in the woods or head up a mountain without telling someone where I was going first. It's just common sense. I'm sure your mom will appreciate it, too."

Scott is the best, Lucy thought.

The pair was so busy searching the work surfaces for paper and a pen that they never heard the elevator doors close and open again, nor saw the movement of two small figures. Lucy and Scott spent the next few minutes huddled together, trying to compose the perfect note. "There!" Lucy exclaimed with satisfaction. "That should do."

She read it over again—silently:

Dear Mom and Dr. Hartwick,

I overheard your conversation about the threats to the time machine. I know you're going to destroy the machine soon, Dr. Hartwick. I can't let you do that without trying to save my dad first.

Scott and I are going to use the time machine to take a quick trip back to April 2064. If all goes well, maybe we'll be back with Dad before you even get a chance to read this. If it takes longer than I think, then please keep the time machine running and the antimatter flowing!

Love, Lucy

"Looks good," declared Scott. "Let's get going!"

They walked over to the machine and retraced the path they had taken earlier with Dr. Hartwick: through the door in the base, up the ladder, through the trap door, and into the capsule. Lucy hesitated as they approached the seats at the front of the pod.

"You take the pilot's seat," said Scott with a grin. "I don't want you accusing me of trying to play captain on this adventure, too."

Lucy winced. "I hope I've grown up a little since then. But... okay."

She turned to the controls and pressed Power. The panel lit up, and Lucy turned her attention to the Laser Intensity sliderbar. "Okay, I want to set a specific date, so I skip this one, right?" she asked.

"Right," agreed Scott.

They were concentrating so hard that they didn't hear a small scuffling noise at the back.

Lucy took her time to type in the date, 03.31.2064. Then she pushed the AD toggle switch and pressed Enter.

"Slowly and carefully, that's what the doctor ordered," declared Lucy with mild irony.

"Dr. Hartwick would be proud," replied Scott.

Lucy reached over to press Activate, then stopped. "You want to do it?" she whispered.

Scott shook his head. "Nope. I'm here for you, and I will support you to the best of my abilities. But if you aren't absolutely positive about what we're about to do, then stop right now."

Lucy sighed. *He's right*, she thought.

"Okay, I'll be the one to do it. I know—I can just feel it—that this is the right thing to do. But before I press Activate—could I please have just one more kiss for luck?"

"Now *that* I can do," said Scott with enthusiasm.

They leaned toward each other, and Scott's hand gently supported the back of Lucy's neck. Just as their lips touched, the doors of the cabinet at the back burst open, and the twins emerged, laughing hysterically.

"A kiss for luck! How... how romantic," Romi choked out between hoots of laughter.

"They... they can't keep their... hands off each other," Remi agreed with hilarity.

Scott and Lucy stood up, united in fury.

"You spying, little jerks!" shouted Scott.

"Creeps!" yelled Lucy. "How dare you follow us? You're going to be in so much trouble!"

Romi and Remi gave each other knowing looks.

"First you have to catch me!" taunted Remi. He ran back toward the pod cabinets, opened a door, and started flinging out equipment. A trowel hit Scott in the shin, hard.

"Ouch!" he exclaimed, and he and Lucy jumped up and ran toward Remi. Scott reached out a long arm and managed to grab Remi by the collar. Suddenly there was a deep clang from below the pod, followed by whirring and snapping noises. Lucy and Scott froze and looked at one another in horror.

"He didn't... did he?" began Scott.

"I have a very bad feeling about this," Lucy said darkly.

They raced back to the front of the pod, where Romi stood quietly, a sly smile on his lips.

"Move over," muttered Lucy, shoving him roughly aside. She took one look at the monitor and stepped back in horror. "He didn't just press Activate, he messed up the date, too!"

Scott rushed over to Lucy and quickly checked the display. The date glowed, red and ominous: 3.31.753 BC.

Chapter 7

"We're not going back three years, we're going back nearly 3,000 years!" Scott exclaimed. He grabbed Romi by the shoulders. "What were you thinking?" he shouted.

Romi disdainfully plucked each of Scott's hands off his shoulders. "I was thinking that going three years back is hardly worth bothering. I was thinking a real time travel adventure should take us way back, to a really important time in history."

"What's so important about 753 BC?" broke in Lucy.

"Yeah, that's pretty random," agreed Scott.

Romi and Remi stared at them in disbelief.

"Duh," Romi said. "Everyone knows that Rome was founded on April 21, 753 BC. We want to see it from the very beginning."

"Since when did you become such avid historians?" asked Scott with a growl.

"Since our whole lives," replied Remi. "Our mom has been drilling Roman history into us since we were babies." He smiled wistfully. "This trip will really make her appreciate us."

"Forget this," Lucy broke in. "We've got to stop the machine!" She moved to the panel, searching frantically. "Oh no! Dr. Hartwick told us you can't stop the machine once it's been activated!" she wailed.

Scott moved to help her. "Can we override the date?" He tried pressing the keypad buttons, to no avail. "Looks like it's locked in." He rose abruptly and ran to the pod door. He rattled the handle in vain.

"We're locked in, too?" guessed Lucy.

"Yup."

"Well, you wanted this, boys," Lucy said. "Better sit down and strap up, because we're going to take the ride of your lives."

Lucy and Scott quickly buckled themselves in at the front of the pod, while Romi and Remi sauntered over toward the middle row of seats. The pod remained still, and now the only sound they could hear was a faint buzzing.

"Is anything really happening?" complained Romi.

"Shut up!" snapped Lucy. She leaned in to Scott. "Do you think anything's really happening?" she whispered.

"It's powered by antimatter and light, so we're not going to hear much," he answered. "But this timer is definitely counting down to something important." He pointed at a newly lit numerical display next to the Activate button. "It looks like we'll be ready to enter the time loop in 30 seconds!"

A Doorway Through Time

As if in response, the pod began to make a humming noise.

"Right, the pod has an engine just to slip it into and out of the loop," remembered Lucy. She nervously twisted a strand of her hair around her finger. "I wonder if this thing will spin, like our ship did when we went through the wormhole."

"Good evening, and welcome to Roman Airways, Time Travel Flight Double-Oh-One. I'm Romi, and I will be your flight attendant today. The emergency exits are located here, here, here, here, here, here, and here."

Lucy swiveled around in time to see Romi standing in the middle of the pod, arms outstretched, gesticulating wildly. Remi was chortling in his seat. "Sit down, you idiot, and buckle up!" she snarled.

Romi nonchalantly sat down and tugged on his seat belt. "Make sure your seatbelt is buckled low and tight across your lap," he continued in a mock whisper.

Remi stopped laughing long enough to add, "In the unlikely event of a water landing, your seat cushions can be used as flotation devices."

The boys exploded into gales of laughter.

"Knock it off!" roared Scott. "We're about to travel through time, so why are you just fooling around?"

"Calm down," said Romi. "I seriously doubt this thing's going to work."

With perfect timing, the humming sound suddenly

became louder, and the pod began sliding forward. The display was flashing the time 00:00.

"Get ready!" shouted Lucy.

The pod crept forward for a minute, then halted. The humming noise abruptly ended.

"What did I tell you?" asked Romi. "This machine is a failure."

"Whoa, check out Lucy's hair!" interjected Remi. "Nice look, cousin."

Lucy's hair was floating up above her head. She gathered it up and tucked it into her collar.

Something's definitely happening, she thought.

"Zero gravity!" said Scott. "We must have entered the time loop. Watch out for the stuff the twins dumped out of the cabin."

Lucy turned around to see a variety of clothing and equipment bobbing about the pod. Romi and Remi were entertaining themselves by batting a now-weightless flashlight back and forth. "I wish we could see outside," she murmured.

"There's probably nothing to see but blinding light," answered Scott. "But look, the timer is counting down again. Maybe it's counting the minutes we have left to travel."

Lucy focused on the timer as it counted down from five minutes. Scott reached for her hand, and they waited, ignoring the noise behind them. When the timer reached

30 seconds, the humming noise began again in the pod. "You must have been right, Scott. It sounds like the pod is gearing up to take us out of the time loop," Lucy said with relief.

When the timer reached the 00:00 mark, the pod began moving backward. Objects that had been hovering in the air crashed noisily to the floor.

"Oof!" cried Romi as the flashlight he'd been playing with whacked him on the ear.

Good, thought Lucy. *Serves you right.*

That's a bit heartless, cousin, said a voice in her head.

"What!" exclaimed Lucy, turning to look back at the boys. They wore blank expressions.

"Do you think it's safe to get up yet?" asked Remi.

"The seatbelt light is still on," answered Romi.

Lucy looked up.

"Got you, Lucy," Romi said with a smirk.

"We won't get up until the pod stops moving," Scott directed.

The pod slid backward for a few more seconds then came to a halt. The humming died down and ceased altogether. The door automatically slid open.

"Looks like it's time," said Lucy. She and Scott unbuckled and stood up, while the twins jumped up and pushed one another in their anxiety to get out first.

Romi stood still just outside the pod, a bewildered expression on his face.

73

"Where are we?" Remi asked in astonishment.

Lucy pushed them aside and looked around, trying not to betray her own surprise at the changed surroundings. "Duh," she said, consciously imitating Romi's earlier speech. "Everyone knows that when you travel through time, you don't travel to a new place. We went back to the way this cavern was 3,000 years ago."

The metallic room they were in just minutes earlier had been replaced by a gigantic, natural cavern. Huge, milky stalactites dripped from the ceiling, mirrored by creamy stalagmites rising from the floor. The cavern walls were studded with natural crystals that sparkled in the light, adding to the mysterious beauty of the place.

"Whoa," Scott breathed in appreciative amazement as he joined the group.

"Wha-what's that, Lucy?" asked Remi, pointing a trembling finger.

Lucy looked in the direction he was pointing. She could see a gleaming mass of light pulsing behind the pod. It stretched from floor to ceiling and was nearly as wide as it was tall. "It almost looks alive," whispered Lucy.

Remi whimpered, *I'm scared, Lucy.*

You... can talk telepathically! Lucy thought in astonishment. *So you're the one who spoke to me in the pod!*

Must have been Romi, replied Remi. *We've always been able to talk to each other like this. I thought it was a twin thing.* He grinned. *It comes in handy when we're*

74

pulling off a practical joke.

"Well, don't be scared by that glowing thing," Lucy continued aloud, surprised by a sudden maternal feeling for him. "That must be the time loop, Remi, that's going to take us home now." She grabbed Remi's hand, and began dragging him toward the pod.

"What do you mean 'go back home' now?" asked Remi, digging his heels into the cavern floor. "Aren't we going to explore first?"

"This is not the mission I planned to go on," Lucy stated. "We're going to go back home and start over."

Remi looked crestfallen but said nothing.

"What are you talking about?" interrupted Romi. "We just traveled back 3,000 years, and you don't want to see the founding of Rome?"

"I'm sure it would be very educational and all, but..." Lucy trailed off as she noticed the confused expression on Scott's face. "Don't you agree with me, Scott?"

"Umm..." he hesitated, then continued, "Actually, I think this is the single most amazing thing any human being has ever done. Traveling back in time 3,000 years is maybe even more incredible than going through a wormhole. What if we go back home and we get caught? The machine will be destroyed, and nobody will have used it for any good purpose."

Lucy's shoulders slumped. "But my dad..."

Scott put a comforting arm around her waist. "Think

of it this way, Luce. We've arrived at an extraordinary point in human history. I think we owe it to Dr. Hartwick and your mom and the rest of the team to check out ancient Rome. Maybe if we do a good job observing and reporting back, it will convince Dr. Hartwick that the time machine is too important to destroy."

Lucy nodded. "Dr. Hartwick does pretty much worship the great god Research." She leaned into Scott's shoulder. "And maybe our reward could be another trip, this time back to 2064."

"Maybe Dr. Hartwick would even help us with that trip," suggested Scott.

Lucy sighed and slowly stood. "So the vote is...?"

"Stay," said Romi and Remi in unison.

"Stay," Scott agreed.

"Okay then," replied Lucy. "Let's go see if the team packed anything for a trip to ancient Rome."

They headed back into the pod and opened the doors to the storage room. It was a small, shelved space, lined floor to ceiling with boxes.

"Look, they're labeled with dates," pointed out Remi. "This one says '15,000 BC'." He pulled off the lid and peered inside. "Ooh, furry caveman clothes!"

"Keep looking," said Scott. "What are you holding, Romi?"

Romi turned the box, searching for a label. "Oh, here it is," he said. "October 1922. What's the big deal about that date?"

"Dr. Emerson is interested in the rise of fascism," remembered Scott. "He was talking to me about researching the events when Italy's King Emmanuel turned over power to Mussolini."

"Well, that's not going to help," remarked Lucy. "Let me look."

Remi backed out of the way, and Lucy reached for a large box on the bottom shelf. She dragged it out and read the label on the lid. "753 BC!" she exclaimed in delight. "Looks like someone else had the same idea!"

"Well of course they did," Romi disdainfully replied. "Anyone intelligent who could travel back in time to Italy would want to see 753 BC."

"Yeah, I get it, you're smart and I'm stupid," Lucy replied with irritation. She opened the lid of the box and paused for a moment in amazement. She picked up an object from the box and held it up. "They wore leather headbands?"

To Lucy's surprise, Romi and Remi both turned red. *What's the big deal?* she wondered.

"You tell her what the big deal is," said Romi.

"Well, um, that's just f... for women," stuttered Remi.

"So what, women still wear headbands," retorted Lucy. Still mystified, she turned the band around in her hands.

"Lucy, I think that's some kind of, uh, bra," explained Scott in a low voice.

77

"Oh, I see," said Lucy, finally understanding the twins' embarrassment.

Lucy dug deeper into the box and pulled out another garment that she held in front of Romi's midriff. "Perfect—leather underpants! And it looks like they're just your size."

"That's a subligaculum," answered Romi in a strangled voice. He turned an even deeper red, if possible.

Lucy caught Scott's eye, and they burst out laughing.

"You know, I certainly don't plan to take off any clothes while we're out exploring," Scott said. "Why don't we skip being historically accurate and keep our own underwear?"

"Good idea!" agreed Remi. "Now, do you think we should wear togas over our tunics, Romi? It might be too warm for nearly April."

"Well, let's take a look at what we've got," Romi answered. He reached into the box and pulled out an armful of garments, which he dumped unceremoniously on the floor.

"Wool," he pronounced with disappointment. "We're going for the rustic look."

"What else is there?" wondered Scott.

"Oh that's right, you don't know anything," replied Romi, his confidence fully restored. "At this point in time, there are Etruscans camped out on the north side of the Tiber River—you know, the big river that cuts through Rome?" he said with deliberate slowness.

A Doorway Through Time

"We're not infants, Romi. And yes, even stupid me has heard of the Tiber River," Lucy interrupted.

"Excellent!" continued Romi. "So the Etruscans are recent immigrants who've settled on the eastern side of the river, and these guys have linen clothes and gold jewelry and some pretty nice art. The Latins, meanwhile, aren't quite so sophisticated. They're herding sheep and camping out on the southern side of the river. I'm sure there are a lot of different tribes in the region, like the Sabines even further north, but the Etruscans and the Latins are the big ones."

"Latins—so they speak Latin?" asked Scott.

"Good job, genius," retorted Romi.

"I don't see how we're going to communicate with these people! I haven't studied Latin since high school. What about you, Luce?" Scott asked Lucy.

"I won the Junior Classical League award last year, but it's not like you go around speaking it," she replied.

Remi made a show of clearing his throat.

Lucy turned to him. "Let me guess—you guys were forced to speak Latin at home?"

"Oh yeah," Remi nodded. "And Italian and Greek..."

"Jeez, it's like you were made for this trip," muttered Scott, turning back to the box of clothing.

Lucy was starting to turn back, too, when she noticed Romi raising an eyebrow at Remi and overheard his thought.

Judith Bourassa Joy

What did I tell you, brother? Even they are starting to see it.

Lucy bent down over the box, still observing Remi out of the corner of her eye. He anxiously put a finger to his lips and jerked his head toward Lucy. She closed her own mind. *Something is definitely up*, she decided. *I've got to keep a close watch on those two.*

"Okay, so what is all this stuff? It looks like some scratchy pillowcases and sheets," she said aloud.

"The pillowcases are tunics. They're what everyone wears," answered Remi. "These are just right—sewn up the sides and on the top, with holes for our heads and arms. Uh, Lucy, do you mind?"

"What? Oh yeah," said Lucy, taking a tunic and heading out of the pod. "You guys can change inside. I'll dress outside by the light of the time loop."

Lucy closed the pod door and shed her pants and shirt. She pulled the tunic on and grimaced as she saw her reflection in the pod. *I'm wearing a sack*, she thought. She grabbed her 21st-century clothes and pounded on the pod door. "Little pigs, little pigs, let me come in!"

The door slid open, and Lucy laughed at the three boys. "You look as awful as I do!"

"Who cares what we look like!" retorted Romi. "But we should wear belts, too." He reached into the box and pulled out four leather belts. They were about three inches wide, with long leather laces. "Put the belt around your

80

waist and tie it in front with the laces," he explained. "Then you kind of pull on the top of your tunic to make it puffy and to make it shorter, if you need to—it should come about halfway down the calves of your legs."

"How do you know all this?" asked Lucy in amazement.

"Mom has made us go to way too many classics festivals," replied Remi, shaking his head. "And she always makes us go in costume."

"Well it's lucky for us that you guys know what to do with this stuff," said Scott. "What about the togas? Should we wear them? I have no idea how to put them on."

Lucy felt a twinge in her forehead and realized Romi and Remi were having a telepathic conversation. She quickly tuned in.

Togas would be more impressive, Romi was saying.

It might be pretty hot in spring, whined Remi.

I can't expect them to see me as a leader if I don't dress the part, replied Romi. *You know the story—*

She's listening, interrupted Remi.

Romi looked at Lucy and scowled.

They don't know how to close off their minds, Lucy suddenly realized. "Don't worry, Romi," Lucy whispered, feeling sudden sympathy for her young cousin. "I know exactly how you feel. I think you're doing a fine job leading us right now."

Romi looked confused. "Thanks," he answered, turning back to the pile of clothing on the floor. "C'mon Remi, you wrap Lucy's toga, and I'll do Scott's."

It took several minutes to get the togas correctly draped and pinned with the simple bronze brooches Remi found in a corner of the box.

Lucy looked around at the group in satisfaction. "We look great!"

"We're barefoot," said Romi.

"No problemo, brother. Have sandals, will travel." Remi pulled out a pile of leather sandals. "Watch how I lace them up," he instructed.

Remi quickly had the sandals on his feet, with the long leather laces criss-crossed around and up the calves of his legs. With some difficulty, Lucy and Scott followed his example.

"Are we ready now?" asked Lucy.

"Ah... you should put your hair up like my mom's," said Remi, looking critically at Lucy. "There are elastic bands in here you can use. Just cover them up with your hair."

Lucy fumbled with her hair for awhile, then gave up in dismay. "I can't do it! I'm no good at this!"

"I can help you, Lucy," said Scott. "I used to help my mom when she was so sick those last few weeks before she died." He took a bronze comb and gathered Lucy's hair into a chignon, then stuck the comb into the bun to hold her hair in place.

"Thank you," Lucy said softly, leaning in to him.

"Please don't kiss again," interrupted Romi. "I don't

think my stomach can take any more."

Lucy gave Scott a theatrically long kiss in reply, while the twins made retching noises. She broke away from Scott with a smile and checked the box one last time. "We basically don't have any equipment. The only things left are a few daggers. They don't even have sheaths."

"We're supposed to tuck the bare knives into our belts," explained Remi as he chose one from the box.

"Better watch how you bend over," cautioned Lucy as she picked a dagger of her own.

"How about cameras?" asked Scott. "How can we prove we've been here?"

"I still have my contacts in," said Lucy. "I can take photos with those." She automatically touched the small metal disk clipped to the back of her ear. "Good, my computer chip is still attached."

Scott stepped forward. "All right then. Let's grab some flashlights and get out of here! We'll split up and check the walls. Watch for bats—if there's a tunnel that leads aboveground, they'll be using it."

Lucy, telled Remi anxiously, *I m scared of the dark.*

Don't worry, Lucy answered. *I'll stick with you.*

"Let's buddy up, Scott," Lucy directed. "I'll go with Remi."

Half an hour later, Lucy was beginning to doubt they would ever get out when her thoughts were interrupted by gleeful shouts.

"We found it!" chorused Romi and Scott.

Lucy and Remi ran across the cavern to join them.

"That's a big tunnel," Lucy noted. "Good work, guys."

They began the slow climb upward, carefully navigating the jagged, winding path. Lucy forced herself to take slow, deep breaths as the path narrowed. After all, it would have to be pretty small at the surface, or other people would have discovered the cavern, she told herself. And her mom said the cavern was untouched before the team moved in.

Lucy was surprised to feel a small, warm hand in hers.

Don't worry, Lucy, Remi told her. *I'm sure it'll be fine. Your mom wouldn't have built a time machine in that cave unless it had a safe way out.*

"Thanks, Remi," she whispered, giving his hand a grateful squeeze.

Scott stopped so abruptly that Lucy bumped into him. "What's wrong?" she asked.

"We've hit a dead end," answered Romi.

"That can't be possible!" exclaimed Scott. "We saw a bat come out of this tunnel!"

Lucy pushed forward and began frantically feeling the walls of the cavern. Her heart was pounding. *We can always turn back*, she thought. *This isn't a tomb.*

"Wait!" shouted Romi. "It's not what it seems."

Lucy swung her flashlight around and was astonished when Romi seemed to melt into the rock.

84

A Doorway Through Time

"What the—" gasped Scott.

Muffled laughter came from the other side of the wall.

"It's kind of an overhang. There's a gap between the walls, and you can squeeze behind the wall we ran into."

The others quickly followed Romi and gazed in relief at the sight that met them.

"Sunlight," said Lucy happily. She scrabbled up the steep rise at the end of the tunnel and squeezed through the narrow crack in the wall. A bucolic scene awaited her. "Hey!" she shouted. "3,000-year-old sheep!"

Chapter 8
❦ ❦ ❦

They emerged from the tunnel onto a ledge that jutted out over a rock-strewn hillside. At the base of the hill, golden fields of grass extended for miles, dotted with clumps of bushes and small trees. Sheep grazed in clusters, contentedly wagging their tails in circles. The setting sun cast a rosy glow over the scene, and in the distance, Lucy could see a glimmer of silver. "Water!" she exclaimed. "Is that the Tiber?"

"It must be," answered Romi.

"Our view of it was blocked by the mountains circling our valley," Scott said. "We must have completely cut through the hill the villa was built on and come out on the other side."

"I've got to get some pictures," Lucy decided. She blinked twice and said "Camera." Crosshairs floated in front of her line of vision, and Lucy focused on the river without blinking. The scene froze for a second, and she knew a photo had been taken and transmitted from her contact lenses to the chip behind her ear. She continued to take a series of landscape shots and, once satisfied, ordered, "Camera off."

"Where are all the people?" asked Lucy.

"Look for smoke," Scott suggested.

"There," said Romi, pointing a finger to the southwest. "The village must be down there, near the water."

Lucy looked in the direction Romi was pointing and saw a smudge of gray on the horizon. "Okay then, let's go meet the natives!" she declared.

Remi looked nervously at Romi.

"You're not just going to walk right up and introduce yourself, are you?" Romi asked with disdain.

"He's got a point," said Scott thoughtfully. "If there are a lot of different tribes in the area, they aren't likely to be very welcoming to visitors. I think we should observe them in secret for a while."

"Good idea," Remi said quickly.

"Why don't you lead the way," suggested Romi. "Find the best path so that we aren't too obvious. I bet you'd be good at that, being a military officer and all."

Why is Romi sucking up to Scott all of a sudden? Lucy wondered suspiciously.

"Uh, okay," answered Scott in surprise. "Let's head for that cluster of olive trees down there, to our left."

"What about the flashlights?" asked Remi.

"What about them?" Romi asked.

"Well, they really won't fit in here. Maybe we should

leave them behind for the return trip?"

"Good idea," agreed Scott. "We can hide them behind the rock that covers the tunnel entrance."

The four of them hid their flashlights and began picking their way down the hardscrabble hill. When they reached the bottom, they dashed over to a small grove of trees. Panting slightly from their exertions, they heard a far-off whistle. A dark, four-legged shape appeared in the distance, racing toward the nearest group of sheep. The teenagers crouched down behind the trees and peered at the scene.

"The shepherd must be nearby," whispered Scott. "Looks like his dog is bringing the sheep in for the night."

They watched in silence as the dog carefully circled the sheep and drove them toward another group. After a few minutes, a herd of about three dozen sheep had been gathered near the hill, underneath the ledge where the adventurers had stood just half an hour earlier.

A man appeared from behind a nearby stand of thorn trees and leaned down to give the dog a pat. Although the light was fading fast, Lucy could see that the shepherd was swarthy and had a full beard. He held a thick staff in one hand.

"He's only wearing a tunic," Lucy whispered. "Are you guys feeling a little overdressed in your togas?"

"What do you boys think?" asked Scott, turning back to Romi and Remi. "You seem to be the ancient Roman experts."

Romi shrugged nonchalantly. "Not everyone we meet will be a shepherd," he replied in a low voice.

Remi glanced at his brother, then turned toward Lucy and Scott. "We want to make a good first impression when we do meet people. We're keeping ours on."

Suddenly, the sheepdog pricked up his ears and turned toward the hidden group. The shepherd gave a command, and the dog started trotting in their direction.

"He must have heard you!" whispered Romi to his brother. "Now you've messed up everything!"

"How could he have heard us? We're so far away!" exclaimed Remi in astonishment.

"You should know by now that dogs and wolves have amazing hearing," Romi chided.

What's that supposed to mean? thought Lucy.

"We're probably just going to have to go out and introduce ourselves to the shepherd," decided Scott, unaware of the twins' conversation.

"If the dog lets us," Lucy said.

The dog was approaching them at a gallop, growling as it ran.

"Get out your knives, just in case," said Scott. "Let's try and scare him off first."

Lucy was just reaching for her knife when the sheepdog stopped short. It raised its nose and sniffed the air. The dog stood stiff-legged and its hackles rose.

"Now what?" she worried.

As if in answer, a chorus of menacing howls filled the air.

"Wolves," stated Romi with satisfaction. "The dog is going to decide the wolves are more dangerous than us. And the dog is right."

Why doesn't Romi look nervous? wondered Lucy.

"Where are the wolves coming from?" Romi asked Remi.

"There," said Remi, pointing to the northeast. A pack of seven wolves were lined up on a high ridge. They seemed to scan the scene before them before swooping down in silent formation toward the sheep.

"They realized the dog has left the sheep unguarded," Scott realized. "This is our fault. I've got to help the shepherd."

They all stood up and ran toward the shepherd. The sheep were no longer in a tight group, but instead were beginning to dash about in different directions, bleating frantically. The wolves descended on the herd and began expertly separating the sheep even farther. Lucy watched in horror as an enormous wolf closed its jaws around a small lamb's head. The wolf gave the struggling animal a quick shake, and the lamb hung limp and silent.

"Broke its neck," said Romi matter-of-factly.

The sheepdog raced ahead with a terrifying snarl and hurled himself at the wolf. The wolf dropped the dead lamb and staggered sideways, nearly falling. The wolf quickly regained his balance, however, and leaped at the dog. Dog and wolf were engaged in a deadly wrestling match, twisting and snapping at one another. The shepherd, meanwhile, was farther back, shouting and beating another wolf with his staff.

"You guys stay back!" shouted Scott. "I don't want you getting hurt."

He headed for a nearby wolf that was harassing a heavy, slow-moving sheep and began shouting and slashing at the wolf with his knife.

"Do what he says!" Lucy called to the boys. "I'm going to help the dog!"

"Be careful!" cried Romi in alarm. "Make sure you don't hurt the wolves!"

"Thanks so much for your concern!" Lucy quipped.

She put all thoughts of the twins aside and focused on the scene before her.

If this were a dogfight, she thought, *Dad would tell me to grab one of them by the back legs and pull.*

The dog and the wolf were reared up on their hind legs grappling one other, each trying to pierce the other's jugular vein. Lucy leapt at the feet of the wolf and grabbed its back legs, pulling hard. The wolf slammed to the ground, gasping for breath. The sheepdog fell on all fours in surprise, gave Lucy a quick, appraising look, then ran off to drive away another wolf. Lucy scrambled to the front of the wolf and used all her weight to hold its head firmly against the ground. She raised her knife over the wolf's neck, prepared to strike. The wolf rolled its eyes back to look at her and whined. Lucy's raised hand trembled. *I can't kill it. It looks too much like a dog.* She quickly grazed the wolf's neck with her knife and began shouting. "I warned you. Now get out of here! Git! Git!"

She released the wolf and the animal rose, its sides heaving, and clumsily clambered to its feet. It hesitated, then started toward her.

"I mean it! Get out!" Lucy shrieked. She waved her arms and brandished her knife, and to her immense relief, the wolf turned around. The wolf had just broken into a gallop when it suddenly stumbled and yelped in pain. It soon recovered, however, and gamely headed toward the ridge, limping as it ran.

The shepherd paused in his fight to raise a horn to his lips. He blew urgently into the horn, and the sound swelled and echoed over the fields. He turned back to the fight, as did Lucy, and the three humans and dog continued to assail the remaining wolves. After a few minutes, Lucy was dimly aware of the arrival of other men, but the scene was a confusing blur of sounds and sights. The air was filled with the piercing cries of bleating sheep, punctuated by the shouts of men and the sheepdog's barks. The sheep charged about, constantly shifting direction, so that it was difficult to move. Lithe, dark bodies moved effortlessly through the hubbub, silently and efficiently attacking the weakest sheep. After what seemed like hours, but was actually a matter of minutes, the wolves slipped away. The grass was wet with blood.

"Lucy? Are you okay?" called Scott.

"Just a few nicks," she answered. "And you?"

"I'll be okay," he answered, running to her side.

The other men began shouting too and headed menacingly toward Lucy and Scott.

"Can you make out what they're saying?" asked Scott.

"I don't think they're coming to say thank you," muttered Lucy.

The shepherd reached them first. "Quisnam es vos? Quis es vos effectus hic?" he demanded.

"I think he's asking who we are?" Lucy ventured.

"Yeah, I think so, too," answered Scott. "Romi and Remi could tell us for sure. Wait—where are they?"

They looked about, ignoring the shepherd. Lucy closed her eyes and concentrated, but could not pick up the twins' thoughts. "They must have run off. I can't see or sense them. If they were in trouble, I think I could tell."

"That's good," said Scott in relief. "One less thing to worry about. Why don't you try and talk to these guys."

"What do you mean? You've had one more year of Latin than me."

"Yeah, but you're the great communicator."

Lucy sighed, and in her very best public school Latin,

addressed the shepherd and other men who now encircled them. "I am Lucy and this is Scott. We are travelers."

"You distracted my dog!" shouted the shepherd in return. "It's your fault I'm missing five lambs, and many more sheep are wounded."

One of the men came close to Lucy and touched her hair. Another pushed forward and stroked her arm. The smell of dirt and sweat was overpowering, and Lucy had no doubts as to what they were thinking.

"No touch!" Scott demanded.

The men paused in their attention to Lucy, and several chuckled at Scott's rudimentary Latin. Another man, somewhat taller and heavier than the others, raised his staff. Before Scott could react, the cudgel came down on the back of his head. Scott fell silently to the ground.

"Scott!" shrieked Lucy. "Move!" she ordered as she shook off groping hands and kneeled over Scott. She put a finger to Scott's neck and felt his strong pulse. "Thank goodness," she whispered.

There was a sudden, sharp pain in her head, and the world went dark.

Chapter 9

꙳ ꙳ ꙳

Meanwhile, the twins watched the fight's progress from the safety of an olive tree.

"What're we waiting for, Romi?" complained Remi. "I feel like we should be down there helping."

"Whose side are you on?" asked Romi. "This will be good for you, too."

Remi flushed. "Sorry," he mumbled.

Mollified, Romi continued. "I don't know exactly what I'm waiting for. But I'll know it when I see it." He pointed at Scott, who had stumbled and was now fending off a wolf's sharp attack. "Looks like Scott's going to have some nasty bite marks."

"Whoa, check out Lucy," said Remi. She had just jerked a wolf to its feet and was holding her knife aloft.

"What the—" began Romi. "She's letting it go!"

The boys watched in astonishment as the wolf loped away, limping as it ran.

"This is what I was waiting for," said Romi with authority. He swung himself down from the tree branch. "I'm going to follow the wolf. You go over there and grab the dead lamb the wolf dropped. Then hurry up and join me."

"Oof!" grunted Remi, landing less gracefully than his brother. "Why should I have to touch it?"

"Because I said so," answered Romi with finality.

"Oh fine," muttered Remi, seeing the murderous look in his brother's eyes.

While Remi waited for the right moment to run out and steal the lamb, Romi began following the injured wolf as closely as he dared. He dashed from one cluster of brush to another, squinting to keep the wolf in view in the fading light. A soft wind blew gently against his face.

It's a good thing I'm downwind of him, thought Romi. *I can get pretty close without him smelling me.*

Where are you, Romi? called Remi telepathically.

Romi looked back to see his brother several hundred feet behind him. *Over here, by the hemlock trees*, he answered. He leaned away from the trees to wave at his brother, then quickly returned to his hiding spot.

The wolf was traveling very slowly now, its limp more pronounced. Romi waited impatiently for Remi to join him. At last, Remi reached him, panting heavily.

"Got it," he said, dangling the carcass in front of his brother.

"You can hang on to it for now," Romi said coolly.

Remi made a face. "I was afraid you'd say that."

Romi gestured toward the wolf. "It's nearly worn out.

This lamb will be our peace offering."

"When are you going to give it to him—right now?" asked Remi.

"No, we're going to keep following him until he collapses. It should be soon."

The brothers cautiously followed the slow-moving wolf for several minutes. The wolf headed toward a rocky outcrop and vanished from sight. Romi paused for a moment, thinking.

"What are you waiting for?" asked Remi. "Let's go before we lose him."

"No, wait," ordered Romi. He grabbed Remi's toga and pulled him back.

"What are you doing?"

"I don't think the wolf is going any farther. And we shouldn't try to get too near him until we've rubbed ourselves with the dead lamb. Go on," urged Romi, "Rub the wool all over yourself."

"You've got to be kidding me!" exclaimed Remi. "Why should I do that?"

"We don't want to smell like humans. We want to smell like a sheep, so we don't scare off the wolf. Here, give me that," Romi said impatiently. "I'll go first."

Romi grabbed the dead lamb and rubbed it against his arms, legs and belly. He buried his face in the wool for a moment, then stroked the top of his head with it. He pretended not to notice his brother, who was making faces and fake retching noises all the while.

Romi held out the lamb to his brother. "Rub my back with it. Be careful not to get any blood on my toga. There's just a little blood on the sheep, where it was bitten around the neck."

"Do I really have to?"

"Yup. And you're next."

Remi grudgingly took the lamb and ran the wool against Romi's back.

"Thanks. Now I'll do you."

Remi took care of Romi's back, then shoved the lamb toward this brother.

"Finish getting the scent on the rest of you," he ordered.

With a sigh, Remi took the carcass and slowly began rubbing the lamb against his arm.

"Hurry up, or I'll do it for you. And I won't worry about getting blood all over you."

"All right, all right," Remi grumbled, hastening to finish the job.

After a minute, Remi was ready, and the two boys raced across the field to the boulders. They found the wolf nestled among the rocks, lying on its side and licking a paw. When it saw the boys, the wolf attempted to rise, but yelped in pain and collapsed.

"It's a girl," Remi whispered. "Look at her belly. You can tell she's been nursing her pups."

A Doorway Through Time

Perfect, answered Romi. He dropped down on all fours, the dead lamb still gripped in one hand. He began making whimpering noises and shuffled toward the wolf.

What the—? Remi tellied.

I'm trying to sound like a wolf pup, so she isn't scared of me, answered Romi.

The wolf pricked up her ears, interested and alert. Romi stopped several feet short of her and slowly removed his knife from his belt. The wolf gave a threatening growl. Romi froze in place and resumed whimpering, and the wolf stopped growling. Romi quickly sliced a chunk of flesh from the lamb's shoulder and tossed the meat to the mother wolf. She sniffed it warily, eyed the brothers for a moment and then snatched up the meat. In one gulp, the food was gone. Romi cut a larger hunk of meat from the lamb's thigh, moved a little closer and pushed it forward. Just as the wolf was reaching for the food, Remi started toward his brother. The wolf immediately stiffened.

Get down on all fours, Remi, ordered Romi. *Then don't move.*

Once Remi got down, the wolf relaxed again. The brothers watched as she hungrily shredded and swallowed the second piece of meat.

Now you do it, said Romi. He sawed a third slice of meat from the rump.

Remi hesitantly crawled forward and took the bloody piece from Romi. With trembling hands he tossed it to the

99

wolf. *Gross*, he thought.

Once the wolf had finished, Romi crawled toward her and held the mutilated carcass out with both hands. The wolf looked Romi straight in the eyes, appraising him. Romi met her stare for a second, then looked away and lay down on the ground, belly up. The wolf's tail thumped the ground, and she briefly licked Romi's hand. Then she snatched up the lamb and began gnawing away, accepting both the offering and the boy.

Being submissive suits you, brother, thought Remi. He couldn't repress a grin.

Shut up, answered Romi, *You're going to have to do this, too. In fact, lie down right now and come join me.*

With a sigh, Remi lay on his belly and slithered toward his brother.

Romi rolled over onto his belly to watch the wolf as she ate. *Take a look at this. She's got some bite marks and scratches. But it looks like they'll heal okay on their own. Why do you think she's limping?*

It must be her feet, answered Remi. *She was licking one when we got here. Let me take a look.*

Remember to whimper if you want to get really close, Romi reminded him.

Right.

Remi wiggled forward, whining like a puppy. The wolf began wagging her tail again. Her attention was focused on the bloody lamb leg. Remi stared hard at the wolf's front paws and finally discovered the problem. *It's a thorn,* he told his brother. *She's got a giant thorn stuck in between her pads.*

Whoa, just like Androcles and the lion. Pull it out and we'll be fine! urged Romi.

Easy for you to say.

Think.

Whatever.

Assessing how best to grasp the thorn, Remi gave a quick glance at the wolf, who was busy trying to tear a particularly tough tendon from the bone. *It's now or never,* he decided.

Remi swiftly reached forward and snatched the base of the thorn. The wolf yelped as he tore the thorn from her paw. She leaned forward and grabbed his wrist in her jaws. Remi felt the pressure of her sharp canine teeth, which could easily sever his arm. He began whimpering again, and directed the force of his telepathic thoughts at the wolf. *I'm trying to help you,* he explained. *See the thorn?*

The wolf released her grip and sniffed at the thorn. She looked up at Remi, staring unblinkingly at him with her amber eyes. Remi met her gaze for just a moment and then looked down. He rolled over onto his back and whined. The wolf sniffed his face and finally licked his forehead.

She likes me, too! Remi said telepathically.

That's it, then. We're nearly ready to start a legend, Romi answered.

The wolf resumed licking her paw, and Romi and Remi looked in vain for something to eat. The wolf had eaten most of the meat from the bones, but the entrails spilled out of the lamb's belly. "Should we try eating that stuff she didn't want?" whispered Remi.

"I'm not that desperate," Romi answered. "If we go to sleep, we won't notice we're hungry. Of course, we're supposed to drink wolf milk, but..."

Romi and Remi both looked unhappily at the wolf's belly. "Let's not and say we did," Romi said finally.

"Works for me," answered Remi. "I'm ready to try sleeping instead."

The boys took off their togas and wadded them up into makeshift pillows. They brushed away the bigger pebbles and lay down gingerly on the hard soil.

"This is really uncomfortable," complained Remi.

"It doesn't bother her," whispered Roemi, jerking his head toward the wolf.

The wolf had finally finished licking her paw and was now stretched out fast asleep, snoring gently.

"Great, first a lumpy bed and now we have to listen to snoring, too," murmured Remi.

"I have to listen to you snore every night."

"Shut up!"

Remi began pummeling his brother, who started punching him back. The wolf woke with a snort and raised her shaggy black head. She growled menacingly at the brothers, who quickly stopped fighting.

"Sorry, uh—" apologized Remi. "Hey Romi, what're we going to call her?"

"She's our new mother now," Romi replied calmly. "Let's call her 'mother' in Latin— 'matris'."

"I don't know," said Remi dubiously. "It doesn't really sound good. Isn't there another way to say it— 'genetrix'?"

"How is that better than matris?"

"We could shorten it to Genny— like 'Jenny', but with a 'G'. That sounds nice."

"Matris."

"Genny."

"Matris."

Remi pouted. "Listen, Romi, you get to be king. You get to be the one everyone cares about in the history books. Let me name the wolf!"

Romi sighed. "Oh all right. Nobody knows the name of the wolf, anyway." He inclined his head toward the wolf. "We'll be quiet now, mother Genny."

The wolf gave a snort and lay her head back down. Soon she was snoring gently again, and the boys, exhausted from their adventure, both fell into deep, dreamless sleep.

Chapter 10

Lucy awoke to a splitting headache. She tried to stretch but realized she couldn't move her upper body. The light was dim, and smoke created a disorienting haze, but she discovered the source of her troubles—she was tied tightly to a wooden pole in a large, one-room hut. She was seated on bare ground, and her outstretched legs were bound at the feet. She could feel the body of another person against her back.

"Scott?" she whispered. When there was no answer, she wriggled as much as the tight bonds would allow, then tried again in a slightly louder voice. "Scott! Is that you?"

Scott groaned and shifted slightly. "Lucy?"

"Scott, we're tied up in some hut. My head's killing me, and I don't think it's because I'm having a telepathic moment."

"My head hurts, too. And I'm definitely not becoming telepathic."

"The last thing I remember is seeing this big, nasty dude hit you on the back of your head, hard, with his staff.

They must have done the same thing to me."

"That explains the headache. Think they could give us some Ibuprofen?" he joked weakly.

"Seems very likely. After all, they've been so kind to us already."

There was movement in a dark corner of the hut, and a figure turned toward them.

"Exsisto quietis!" the woman screeched. "Be quiet!"

"Did you get that?" Lucy whispered.

"Yeah, she wants us to shut up," he whispered back.

Lucy blinked twice and murmered, "Camera." She surveyed the room, snapping photos as far as her head could turn in each direction. As her eyes adjusted to the dim light, she could see that the hut was oval in shape, with walls covered in a gray plaster. Every few feet, rough posts supported the walls. Posts bisected the structure to hold up the thatched roof. Lucy and Scott were bound to a pole near the back of the hut, opposite the entrance, and because she was facing the wooden door, Lucy could see the whole space. A fire burned inside a ring of stones near the center of the building, and a hole in the roof inefficiently served as a chimney.

The door swung open, letting in a shaft of light that nearly blinded Lucy. A man entered, grunted something at the woman, and walked toward Lucy. Unlike the shepherd, he was wearing a toga and carried himself with authority.

The boys were right, thought Lucy. *I'm glad I'm*

105

dressed as well as he is.

The man crouched down next to Lucy and stroked her cheek. "Mollis," he said in a deep voice. "Soft."

Oh no! she thought.

His eyes raked over Lucy's body—appraising her. He reached out to stroke her face again, but this time his hand continued down past her neck. He was nearly to her chest when Lucy struck. She twisted her body and swung her bound legs as hard as she could against his shins, managing to knock the man down. With a roar of anger, he rose up and slapped Lucy hard. Blinking back the tears, she looked defiantly in his eyes. *I will not let him see me cry.*

Just then a piercing howl rent the air. The man swiveled his head toward the woman in the corner, momentarily forgetting about Lucy.

"How is he, Tatiana?" he asked in Latin.

"Tullius is worse than ever, Marius, as you could have seen if you weren't so interested in that—that girl," the woman replied angrily. "He is burning up with fever."

The man quickly rose and strode toward the woman. She moved aside, and Lucy could see a baby writhing unhappily on a fur blanket on the floor. Lucy furiously tried to combine her keen sense of intuition with her recollection of Latin vocabulary. The man tenderly reached out a hand to feel the child's forehead. "You speak truly," he admitted. "I don't see how he can survive. So many strong men in our village have already died."

A Doorway Through Time

Tatiana put her hands to her face and began sobbing. Marius wrapped his arms around her and murmered words that Lucy could not overhear. She took advantage of the situation to whisper to Scott. "They've got a sick kid. It sounds like a lot of people around here are sick, too."

"That's what I thought I heard them say, too," Scott answered. "I wonder if it's something I could help them with? I mean, I am pre-med, after all. I've learned a lot of stuff already as a paramedic, too."

"Great idea!" Lucy exclaimed. She cleared her throat, and Marius and Tatiana looked up at her. Resentment burned in Tatiana's eyes. "We can help you," Lucy said in her best Latin. "My friend is a healer."

"Our own healer has been able to do nothing," Tatiana replied fiercely. "Why would your friend be any better?"

"We are foreigners," Scott answered. "We have new ideas that will help."

Marius narrowed his eyes and crossed his arms, thinking. "If you save his life, I will spare yours," said Marius.

Scott twisted to face Marius. "And you will leave my woman alone," he demanded.

Marius hesitated and Tatiana jumped in. "Yes, she will be all yours, and after you save my son, you will leave this village forever."

"Tatiana..." Marius began in a warning voice. "You know it is my right as chief to keep her. The men would think me weak if I did not." He turned back to Scott. "You will save my son, and I will set you free forever. But your woman is mine."

"Then I will not help you," Scott countered. "You can kill me, and your son will die."

Marius stamped his foot and growled in frustration. The baby began whimpering.

To Lucy's surprise, Tatiana stepped in front of her husband so that she stood between him and Lucy. The tiny woman was quivering with anger. "Your son's life is at stake!" she cried. "You would let Tullius die instead? Let this man save our son, then send the foreigners away from our village. We don't want them here."

Marius stared fiercely back at his wife and raised a hand to strike her. Tatiana met his gaze unflinchingly. Marius hesitated, then dropped his hand and, to Lucy's surprise, chuckled softly. "I have always loved your spirit, Tatiana."

His eyes softened and he stroked her hair lovingly for a long moment. Then, suddenly remembering his hostages, he looked up and spoke in a business-like voice. "If you save my son's life, you and your woman are free to go. No man in my village will touch her. But if you fail, you will be executed, and she is mine."

"Very well," said Scott. "Now unbind us, and I will examine your son."

Marius drew a short blade from his belt and swiftly cut the ropes that held Scott to the pole and bound his feet.

With a groan, Scott stood up and rubbed his sore wrists.

"Uh, Scott?" inquired Lucy.

"Lucy, too," Scott said to Marius, nodding in Lucy's direction. "I need her help."

Marius looked suspiciously at Scott for a moment, but slowly knelt down to cut Lucy's bonds. He made a point of running a finger along her back as he made his way to her bonds, and it took all of Lucy's willpower not to punch him. Finally, Marius cut the cords around Lucy's wrists and feet. She stood up and was pleased to be several inches taller than him.

"Move aside, buster," she said in English, enjoying seeing the confusion in his eyes.

Scott was already kneeling on the ground, examining the baby. Lucy hurried to join him, with all the dignity she could muster. Scott looked anxious.

"What do you think?" she whispered.

"I'm not sure yet," he answered.

"Yeah, well, our lives are riding on this," Lucy retorted. "No pressure."

Scott scowled. "That doesn't help."

Lucy sighed. "Sorry. What can I do?"

"Be quiet and let me think."

Lucy grimaced, but watched silently as Scott palpated the baby's abdomen. Tullius moaned in pain, and Tatiana made a movement toward Scott. To Lucy's surprise, Marius intervened, gently pulling his wife back and keeping his arm protectively around her.

"He's got a fever, he's sweating, and his belly hurts." Scott glanced up at Marius and Tatiana, surveying them with a professional eye. "His parents are olive-skinned, but even so, he looks a little yellow. I think he may have a bit of jaundice."

"Jaundice? So we should just put him outside in the sunshine? They had to put me under a special light when I was born," offered Lucy.

"No, it's not the kind of jaundice newborn babies get. For one thing, he's at least a year old, and for another, he's got a fever."

Tullius shivered with a sudden chill and stiffened. His limbs jutted out at odd angles.

"What's wrong!" exclaimed Lucy in fear.

"He's got rigors, too," answered Scott. "These little seizure-like things when he stiffens up."

He turned to Tatiana and summoned up his best Latin. "Is he eating?"

She shook her head in reply. "He ate a little yesterday, but threw it up soon after."

"Fever, chills, rigor, abdominal pain, jaundice... Think, Scott, think!" Scott said aloud to himself.

"Are the other sick people in the village like this?" he asked Marius.

"Yes," Marius replied. "It is always the same. And after a week or so, they fall into a sleep that they never wake up from..." his voice trailed off.

Scott stood up. "Let me see your village," he said with authority.

Surprised, Marius moved toward the door and swung it open. Scott strode through, followed closely by Marius. Trailing a few steps behind them, Lucy began taking photos of the scene before her. The village was comprised of about thirty skin tents and a dozen huts, clustered on a flat plain near the Tiber River. The huts were all roughly oval in shape, like the one that had confined Lucy and Scott. On the far side of the village, several men were busily at work constructing a new building. Lucy could see that between each vertical support post ran a network of branches that the men were slathering with what looked like mud.

"Wattle and daub," said Scott, interrupting her thoughts. "They haven't figured out yet that bricks are stronger and less flammable."

"I thought ancient Rome would be filled with marble halls and statues," she confessed.

"Someday it will be, but that will take awhile. Check out all the tents—they're just getting this village started."

Lucy gazed back toward the river and drew in a deep breath. "It smells kind of salty."

"They haven't dammed the river yet. It must still be tidal, and..." Scott stopped to swat a mosquito.

Lucy was scratching a bite of her own. "Look, Scott, it's pretty marshy near here. They must get a ton of mosquitoes."

"That's it!" Scott shouted.

Two men working on the new hut paused to stare. Lucy could feel Marius's questioning eyes on them, too, but she was too excited to care.

"What's it?" she asked urgently.

"It's the mosquitoes. All the symptoms make sense! I know what's wrong with the villagers now." Scott turned to Lucy with a triumphant look. "Malaria. The mosquitoes are infecting them with malaria."

"You're amazing!" Lucy said with a mixture of admiration and relief. "So what's the cure?"

"The classic treatment is some form of quinine," he said slowly.

Why does he look so serious, she wondered.

"So come on, let's find some," Lucy said breathlessly. "Didn't most medicines start out as an extract from some tree or bush?"

"Yes—but Lucy," said Scott, "quinine is native to South America. There's no way it grows around here."

Lucy turned slowly back toward Marius and saw him staring possessively at her. With a shiver she thought, *I'd rather die than belong to him.*

Chapter 11

Lucy began pacing back and forth in front of the chief's hut, trying to think of a way out of their predicament. "Maybe we could just give them something for the symptoms so that they think they've been cured, and then get out of here before they figure it out," she said.

"Like what?" asked Scott.

"Well, I don't know exactly," Lucy answered. "You're supposed to be the expert here. You know, something for the fever. Didn't aspirin come from willow bark originally? There must be willow trees in Italy."

Scott stroked his chin, looking thoughtful. "I don't know if that would be enough to fool them. But it would be a start."

Lucy carefully rubbed the corner of her eye and blinked several times. Her eye began tearing up.

"You okay, Luce?" asked Scott with concern.

"Yes, just something in my contact. I think I got it out, though."

Scott brightened. "Your contacts! They access the memory chip behind your ear. Don't you have some kind of database application stored there, too?"

"Yes," replied Lucy. "So?"

"So maybe you could search for ancient treatments for malaria! There must be something people used in Europe before quinine came on the scene."

"You're right!" Lucy blinked twice and said, "Database search for malaria."

The bucolic scene in Lucy's line of vision melted away and was replaced by a page of text describing the symptoms and causes of malaria. "No, that's not what I want," she muttered. She raised her voice and said, "Search ancient cures for malaria." A page of results appeared, all referring to quinine. Lucy flicked her eyes to the right, scanning through the page and moving on to the next. "Quinine, quinine, quinine," she said with increasing anxiety. "Wait—artemisia?"

"Artemisia?" asked Scott. "What's that?"

Lucy focused on the link and ordered, "Open." After a second, an article appeared before her eyes.

"What do you see, Lucy?"

"It says that thousands of years ago, the Chinese used a plant called artemisia to treat malaria. Looks like it was rediscovered in the 20th century because quinine-resistant strains of malaria began appearing. Scientists extracted artemisin from the plants and found it worked even better than quinine."

"But it's a Chinese plant," Scott said.

"No wait—it actually grows in temperate climates all over the world, in dry areas. And it has lots of names: mugwort, sagebrush, sagewood, wormwood, tarragon, southernwood..."

"Do you have a picture of the plant?"

"Yeah, it looks kind of like the feathery plants I had in my old terrarium," Lucy replied. "It's light green with silvery fuzz on the leaves, and it grows in clumps."

"I'm sure the local doctor must have gathered plenty of plants in the region. Let's go ask him if he's seen it!" exclaimed Scott.

"Close database," Lucy said aloud. The page before her eyes disappeared, and Lucy could see the real world again. "Ready!"

Lucy and Scott hurried over to Marius.

"Where is your healer?" Lucy asked.

Marius looked at her with disdain, then addressed Scott. "What do you want?"

Lucy flushed and started to speak, but Scott put a warning hand on her arm. "We need to talk to your healer," Scott explained.

Marius glanced back at his hut, where the baby's thin cries could be heard. "Very well," he replied. "Come with me. I think he is treating my right-hand man, Secundus."

Marius set off at a quick pace toward a nearby hut, and

Lucy and Scott hastened to keep up. Marius rapped lightly on the door.

"Who goes there?"

"It is I, Marius. I have a foreign healer who wishes to speak with you."

"Wait. Do not enter this house of sickness. I will come to you in a moment."

After a minute, the door opened, and a small, thin man with curly, dark hair stepped outside. His eyes were swollen and red with fatigue, and he swayed a little where he stood.

"Crispus, this is—" Marius paused and looked inquisitively at Scott.

"I am Scott, and this is Lucy."

Marius and Crispus looked puzzled, but Marius collected himself and continued. "They are prisoners. This man claims to know something about medicine. He wants to talk to you about the sickness in our village. He thinks he can help you. His life—and hers—" Marius's cold eyes turned toward Lucy, "depend on it."

Crispus bowed slightly to Marius. "Very well. I need to sit for a moment anyway. Come with me, Sco—" he stumbled over the name, "Scottus and Lucia."

Lucy smiled, and Crispus, tired though he was, smiled wanly in return. "You are in the plains of Latium now, and you must use names we can understand. Now come with me. We will sit in the shade of the olive tree."

Lucy poked Scott in the side. "Let's go, Scottus," she

said with a giggle.

"Whatever you say, Lucia," he returned with a smile. "How come you got the good name?"

They settled down under the olive tree, and Crispus regarded the teenagers with unabashed curiosity. "You are so fair haired, and your accent is so strange. I think Latin is not your first language?"

"Hardly!" replied Lucy in English, with a laugh. She quickly returned to Latin. "No, we are not natives."

"You must be Thracian?" guessed Crispus. "I have heard you are a strange nomadic tribe, whose members have blond or red-gold hair."

"Exactly," said Scott quickly. "We have traveled to many places and met strange people from far-away lands. And we have discovered many new remedies for illnesses."

Crispus's eyes brightened. "Have the gods sent you to save our people?"

"Whoa, this sounds eerily familiar," murmured Lucy in Scott's ear. "Doesn't it... sound like our last... alien... adventure?"

Scott smiled wryly and turned back to Crispus. "Yes," he continued with authority. "We know of an herb that can cure the sickness in this village. I only hope we can find it growing nearby."

"I have made many trips in this region, collecting medicinal herbs," said Crispus with excitement. "What

117

do we need?"

Lucy broke in. "It goes by several names: worm-wood, mugwort, tarragon, sagebrush... Do any of these sound familiar?"

Crispus looked genuinely puzzled. "No, I'm afraid not. But can you describe it?"

"It grows in clusters," Scott said, looking to Lucy for confirmation. "It has thin, feathery leaves that are light green with short, silvery hairs. Lucy can draw it for you."

"I can? Oh, yes, I guess I can," she said in confusion. "What do I draw with?"

Crispus looked up at the branches above them. He broke off a twig, then smoothed a patch of dirt between the roots of the trees. He handed the twig to Lucy.

"With this," he answered.

"I'll try," she said. Drawing on her memory of the photo, Lucy quickly scratched an image in the dirt. Crispus studied it carefully.

"Does it grow in dry places?" he asked.

"Yes!" answered Scott and Lucy together.

Crispus brightened. "I think I have seen it growing on the seven hills over yonder." He pointed at hills several miles in the distance. "Let's go!"

Lucy hesitated, suddenly aware of her intense hunger, and she heard Scott's stomach growl.

Crispus smiled. "Of course, you are hungry. I am as well. I will gather some bread from my house, and we will eat as we travel. It does not do to keep Domino Marius, Chief Marius, waiting."

Lucy and Scott hurried alongside Crispus, who brought them to a small hut in the center of the village. "Please wait outside," he said apologetically. "You may have observed that there are very few women in this village. In fact, I have no woman of my own to keep things clean."

Lucy gave a quiet groan as Crispus disappeared inside the house.

"In case you haven't noticed, it's not exactly an egalitarian society around here," Scott said with amusement.

"Oh, really? No, I hadn't," Lucy replied sarcastically.

Crispus emerged holding a stack of dry bread, which he doled out to them. "I have brought a water skin, too," he told them, patting a leather bag he wore on a strap over his shoulder. "Now we are ready for our journey."

They set off at a good pace, nibbling on the hard wafers and talking. After about an hour and a half, they reached the base of the hills. Crispus pointed at a ravine that rambled up one side of the first hill. "Many interesting plants grow in this sheltered place. It is very dry. Maybe we will be lucky on our first try!"

The three of them fanned out, searching for plants that met Lucy's description. Crispus found a large silver-green plant, but Lucy shook her head. "No, the leaves are much too wide. Our plant is more fern-like."

They searched in vain in the ravine, then checked a

rock-strewn area on a neighboring hill. The afternoon sun was slanting low in the sky, and Lucy was feeling desperate.

"What if we never find it!" she cried in despair.

Scott came over and put a comforting arm around her. "We will. I know we will," he said. He leaned in to kiss her, and Lucy's eyes were just starting to close when she froze, startled by the sudden appearance of a group of five crows taking off in noisy flight nearby.

"We didn't check over there," she said, pointing at the nearby meadow from which the crows had emerged. "Maybe it's a sign."

Crispus brightened. "An omen, did you say?"

They hurried over to the meadow, and began searching with renewed energy.

"Lucy?" Scott called.

Lucy rushed over to see a cluster of plants, sheltered by a ring of boulders. The tall plants had thin, silvery green leaves, with white hairs that sparkled in the sunlight. She turned to Scott and gave him a quick, fierce hug.

"That's it," she confirmed. "Crispus, we've got it!"

They all gathered as much of the herb as they could carry. As they hurried back to the village, Scott and Crispus discussed the best way to administer the medicine, finally deciding to brew a tea from the leaves.

"Be careful," Lucy whispered. "From what I read, it's toxic if you make it too strong."

"I kind of wish you hadn't told me," Scott answered. "I'll just do my best."

Crispus joined them. "What is wrong? I can tell you are worried about something."

"I have never brewed the tea before," Scott admitted. "It is a powerful medicine. If it's too strong, it can kill a person."

"We will not begin with the chief's son, then," said Crispus with a wry smile. "I have a great deal of experience with tinctures of herbs. Let us hope it is enough experience."

Crispus and Scott worked long into the night, preparing a brew that they deemed worthy to test. Scott took a small sip of the final product. "Ugh, it is really bitter," he said with disgust.

"A person can stand a little bitterness if it saves his life," Crispus retorted. "Except—" his voice faltered.

"The baby," Scott said in sudden understanding. "How are we going to get the baby to drink it?"

"We can force it down his throat," said Crispus. "But he may gag it up."

"They always add flavors and sugar to kids' medicine." Lucy's brow wrinkled. "What about honey? Do you have any honey to sweeten it with?"

"Why, yes," answered Crispus, his face lightening. "Very good. We will try it."

Crispus obtained honey from a neighbor, and the three of them set out to treat the villagers. All through the night, Scott and Crispus administered the medicine, while Lucy bathed fevered brows and offered fresh water to wash down the unpleasant dose. Only the chief's son remained.

"Should we try treating the baby now?" Lucy asked.

"Not yet," answered Crispus. "Wait here while I check on our first patient to see how he's doing."

Lucy and Scott waited impatiently for his return.

"What if it turns out we got the wrong plant? What if we actually poisoned them?" Lucy worried aloud.

"We can't think that way, Lucy. We just have to hope for the best."

The sound of running footsteps distracted them. Crispus rushed up and embraced them both. "His fever has broken. Praise the gods!"

"Let's check the others!" said Scott with excitement.

The three doubled back to all the homes they had visited in the night. To their great relief, all the villagers showed signs of improvement.

"Now for Tullius," Crispus directed. "We must be careful with the babe and weaken the dose with water."

"And add plenty of honey," added Lucy.

Crispus and Scott adjusted the medicine accordingly and finally knocked on the chief's door.

"Come in," Tatiana called.

A Doorway Through Time

The three entered and Lucy saw Tatiana still huddled in a corner of the hut, mechanically rocking Tullius in her arms.

"He is so hot and miserable," she said softly, without looking up. "He cannot last much longer."

"We are going to make Tullius better," Crispus assured her.

Tatiana raised her tear-streaked face toward him. "Really? You have found a cure, Crispus?"

"We have, thanks to Scottus and Lucia."

Tatiana gazed wonderingly at the teens. "Forgive me. I doubted you," she said, handing the child to Crispus.

Crispus held the cup of medicinal tea to the child's lips, but the baby turned away, refusing the drink.

"He has never used a cup," said Tatiana. "He is so young, he still suckles."

Crispus and Scott looked at one another in despair. Scott looked over at Lucy.

"Any ideas?" he asked in English. "They aren't going to have any baby bottles around here."

"Let me think," Lucy said as she twirled a lock of her hair around a finger. "Maybe we can make one..."

In sudden inspiration, Lucy reached down and ripped a large strip of cloth from the bottom of her toga.

"He can suck on this. We'll dip it in the tea, then let him suck on the cloth."

Scott nodded. "Good thinking! Let's give it a try."

"Tatiana, maybe you should hold him," Lucy gently suggested.

Tatiana gratefully took her baby, and Lucy handed her the tea-soaked cloth. Tatiana held the material to the child's mouth and tickled his lip with it. To everyone's immense relief, Tullius began to suckle.

"Let me," said Lucy, taking the cup from Scott. Lucy slowly poured a thin, continuous stream of liquid onto the cloth, which the baby continued to suck on. When the tea was gone, Tullius burped loudly and snuggled against his mother.

"He already feels more comfortable," Tatiana whispered in amazement. "Thank you."

"We will stay with you," offered Crispus, "to be sure he improves."

"I know he will," breathed Tatiana. "I thought these foreigners were devils sent to torment me, but now I see that they were gifts from the gods."

Lucy and Scott exchanged glances and grinned.

That's us, thought Lucy. *Saving the universe, one civilization at a time.*

Suddenly, the door to the hut swung open and Marius's short, muscular frame was silhouetted in the weak light of early dawn.

"What news?" he demanded gruffly.

Tatiana turned toward him, her face shining with delight. "Tullius will live, husband! They have saved him."

124

A Doorway Through Time

"The prisoners saved him," Crispus gently interjected. "And thanks to them, all the sick members of our tribe are improving."

"Praise the gods!" Marius exclaimed. He fell to his knees in the doorway and bowed his head as though in prayer, while the others waited in patient silence. Even Tullius was quiet, deep in untroubled sleep. Finally Marius looked up at Lucy and Scott. Scott's arm was around Lucy, and she was leaning unsteadily against him. There was a painful pressure in her head, and she closed her mind as she struggled against waves of exhaustion.

"I have prayed long and often to Apollo, the god of healing," Marius said. "In his great wisdom and mercy, he has answered my prayers. And for the first time, I have heard his voice clearly in my head. Now I know that you, with your hair like the sun"—he nodded at Lucy—"are his daughter, and that you are responsible for saving us."

Lucy looked up at Scott in confusion. *How can this be happening again?* she wondered. *This is too strange a coincidence.*

There was a slight movement in an olive tree outside the hut. Suddenly, Lucy sensed the answer. Quickly, she opened her mind. *Romi? Remi?* she called.

Remi responded, *Hey, cousin, it's Remi, but I've gotta go. My work here is done. See you tomorrow at the party.*

What do you mean? Remi? Answer me! Lucy shouted with her mind.

There was no reply to her questions, and Lucy soon realized Marius was standing in front of her and Scott, speaking to them with his hands outstretched. "Tomorrow we will sacrifice a ram to give thanks to Apollo. Then we will have a feast to celebrate the end of this plague and to thank you, Lucia, daughter of Apollo, and you, Scottus, Apollo's emissary. After that, you are free to leave us, if you wish. If you prefer to stay, you will live among us in honor."

"Thank you, great chief," Scott replied. "We cannot stay here, for Apollo calls us elsewhere." He glanced at Lucy, who was looking very pale. "But it has been a very long night, and now we must rest."

"Of course you must be exhausted," exclaimed Tatiana in concern. "You may use the blankets in the corner and sleep as long as you need."

Lucy quickly replied, "Thank you, but we need to sleep outside, closer to my father, the sun god," She started to rise, and Scott helped her to her feet.

I'm not going to spend another minute trapped in this smoky, smelly hut, she thought as she looked defiantly at Marius.

Marius gave a small shrug. "It is your choice to make."

"And while we're at it," Lucy continued in a firm tone, "we want our knives back."

Marius narrowed his eyes at that and frowned. Tatiana anxiously tugged at his sleeve, but he brushed her off.

A Doorway Through Time

"Now," Lucy reiterated. She stood as tall as she could and glared at him.

"As you wish," he finally agreed.

Marius took their knives from a rough-hewn box at the back of the hut. He bowed stiffly as he presented them. "You may take your blankets now and go," he said ominously.

Marius turned his back on them and regarded his wife, who was wavering with fatigue. He held out his arms and spoke gently to her. "Give me the baby now. You must sleep, too, Tatiana."

That guy has some kind of dual personality, thought Lucy, wondering at the swift change in his voice and attitude.

She and Scott hurriedly stepped outside with their knives back in their belts and two bulky wool blankets. Lucy insisted on sleeping as far from the hut as they dared, beneath an olive tree on the outskirts of the village.

"I heard from Remi. He said he'd see us tomorrow. I'm pretty sure he planted that stuff about Apollo in Marius's head."

"Where is he now?"

"I don't know, he took off in a hurry. Scott, I've just got to lie down."

Lucy flung herself on the ground and pulled the blanket over her. She tucked one arm under her head and patted the ground next to her, inviting Scott to join her. Scott bent down and climbed under the blanket beside her.

"What about Romi?" he asked. "Is he okay, too?"

Lucy, however, could not reply. She was already fast asleep.

Chapter 12
꙳ ꙳ ꙳

Lucy and Scott slept through the night, but all the healthy men in the village had been up before dawn, digging large pits and starting fires in them. At sunrise, six sheep had been slaughtered and gutted. By the time Lucy woke mid-morning, the sheep had been skewered on posts and suspended on support braces inside the pits. Every hour, the carcasses were rotated on their primitive rotisseries to ensure that the meat cooked evenly. Now that the sun was nearly at its zenith, the mutton was completely brown. Fat dripped onto the coals with a sizzling sound, and the smell of roasted meat filled the air with a rich, heady scent.

Lucy and Scott were peering over one of the pits, observing the process, when Lucy felt a gentle tug on her sleeve. She turned to see Tatiana behind her in a deep bow. "Daughter of Apollo, will you test the meat for us to see if it is cooked to your satisfaction?"

News had quickly spread throughout the village about Lucy's supposed godly connection, and the villagers were

129

now treating Lucy and Scott with reverence.

"Gladly, Tatiana. And you don't need to bow to me."

Tatiana looked frightened. "I must not offend the sun god."

"Lucy, just go with it," Scott whispered.

Lucy sighed and accepted Tatiana's offering. "Thank you, Tatiana."

"It had better be cooked all the way through," she muttered in an undertone to Scott. "I bet their sheep have worms."

"Probably," Scott agreed with a grin. "I'm glad I'm not the demi-god here."

Lucy cast him a dirty look and took a delicate bite of the meat. "Oh my gosh, this is delicious!" Lucy exclaimed in delight. She offered the meat to Scott.

"Wow! I was a little dubious about sheep on a stick, but this is fantastic!" agreed Scott.

Lucy turned to Tatiana, who was hovering nearby. "Tatiana, the meat tastes perfect to us," Lucy said in Latin. "Thank you for letting us test it."

Tatiana's face glowed with pleasure. "Very good! I will tell the men to remove the sheep from the fires. While the meat rests, Marius can begin the sacrifice ceremony."

Tatiana hurried off to find Marius while Lucy and Scott walked away from the pits, talking. Lucy shivered a little. "Do you think I really have to watch the sacrifice?" she asked Scott.

A Doorway Through Time

"You know you do," he answered. "And you're going to have to play your part. You can't make faces or look away or do anything but look stoic."

"I don't know if I can watch someone kill an animal right in front of me!"

"You can. And I'll be right there beside you." Scott stopped walking and took both of Lucy's hands in his. "You have an amazing mind. Use it to focus on something else—go somewhere in your imagination and block out reality. That's what they teach us to do in officer training, to help us survive if we get captured in war and tortured. Just put your mind in another place and tune out the sights and sounds of the real world."

"I'll try," Lucy said with a slight tremble in her voice. She leaned in to Scott, who wrapped her in his arms. Lucy was just starting to relax against the warmth of his body, when she felt a tap on her shoulder. She broke away from Scott and turned to see Crispus standing behind her, nervously shifting from one foot to another.

"Dea Lucia, Goddess Lucia, forgive the interruption, but it is time for the ceremony. I was asked to escort you both."

Lucy looked up at Scott in panic. He reached out and gently stroked her cheek.

"You can do it," he whispered.

I'm pretty sure I can do anything if you're with me, thought Lucy. She turned and nodded gravely at Crispus.

"Very well."

They walked in silence for several minutes along a narrow dirt path that led away from the town. Many villagers were ahead of them and behind, solemnly making the same journey.

"Crispus, where are we going?" Lucy finally asked.

"We have a stone altar we use for sacrifices. It is up high, where the gods can see it well."

They walked a little farther, then Scott suddenly stopped. "Lucy, do you see where we're going?" He pointed to a slab of rock jutting out from a nearby hill.

"Is that what I think it is?"

"Yep. Their altar is about a hundred feet below where we came out of the cave. We're going to be very close to the tunnel that takes us to the time machine."

"And home."

Maybe we can create a distraction. Maybe I can get out of this ceremony after all, Lucy thought with excitement. Her pace quickened as her mood improved.

"Lucy," Scott said hesitantly.

"What?" Lucy answered without turning around.

"Wait a minute."

Lucy stopped and turned back to him.

"What's the matter now?" she asked.

"I'm no mind reader, but I can guess what you're thinking. I'm just afraid you've forgotten something important."

What is he talking about? she wondered in confusion.

132

A Doorway Through Time

"Okay. Not something, but someone. Someones."

Oh yeah, the twins, Lucy realized in frustration. *They cause trouble even when they're not around.*

"Well, Remi said they'd be 'at the party.' Maybe something will happen. Maybe we can make something happen."

Scott chuckled. "That's one thing you can count on with those two. When they're around, something always happens."

As they continued their journey, Lucy tried to contact the twins. *Romi! Remi! Are you here? Where are you? Romi! Remi!*

As though from a distance, Lucy heard Romi's voice in her head. *Okay, okay. We hear you! Knock it off!*

Then you should have answered me sooner, she grumbled. *We're going to a sacrificial ceremony near the tunnel to the time machine. It's time to get out of here, and we need you two to join us.*

Don't worry, cousin, we'll join you in our own time.

What do you mean? Romi?

Lucy could no longer hear Romi's telepathic voice. She gave up calling him.

"I heard from Romi," she told Scott in an undertone. "He said they'd meet us at the ceremony, but he won't talk to me anymore. He sounded pretty far away."

"We'll just have to hope they find their way in time. Romi's a smart boy, Lucy. So is Remi."

"Too smart for their own good," Lucy agreed.

Finally, they reached the altar. It was a large, flat rock that had been raised onto four supporting boulders, creating a sort of table. A young white ram with curled horns lay trussed on the altar. It was bleating pitifully, and Lucy's eyes welled up at the sight. *The poor thing*, she thought.

Lucy glanced at Scott. His face betrayed no emotion, but he looked somewhat paler than usual. He felt Lucy's gaze on him and reached out to give her hand a reassuring squeeze.

"They can't have too many rams in the flock or they would constantly be fighting. This poor guy was probably going to be killed anyway. It's too bad they're drawing it out like this, though," he whispered.

Lucy nodded and took a deep breath. She tried turning her attention to the people around her. Every healthy person from the village had gathered, and Lucy saw that there were only a handful of women present. For the most part, the crowd was made up of young adult males, dark and short, dressed in rough tunics. There was a strong smell of sweaty, unwashed bodies and unbrushed teeth, and Lucy wrinkled her nose in distaste. *It definitely gives me a new appreciation for indoor plumbing,* she thought.

Marius stood next to the altar, waiting for the villagers to arrive. While they waited, Lucy tried to reach the twins again, to no avail. Finally, Marius called the crowd to order. "Greetings, one and all!" he shouted.

"Greetings, Domino Marius!" the people dutifully

134

responded.

Marius acknowledged their respect with a small bow of the head, cleared his throat, and continued. "We are gathered here to give thanks to Apollo for delivering us from the plague that has tormented our village. Great Apollo has accomplished his healing through his daughter, Dea Lucia, and her companion, Scottus. In order to show our gratitude, we hereby dedicate the body of this fine young ram to our savior, Apollo. Thanks be to Apollo for saving our village now and forevermore."

Marius raised his right hand, revealing a gleaming silver knife.

"Wait!" called Scott. He pushed his way through to the front of the crowd and confronted the glowering tribal leader.

"What gives you the right to interrupt this sacred ceremony?" demanded Marius.

"You need to understand that this is not the end of the plague. People will continue to get sick if you don't leave your village."

"What do you mean, leave the village?" demanded Marius. "Does Apollo demand that we go on a pilgrimage to his temple?"

"No, you need to get away from the marsh with all its mosquitoes. When they bite you, they give you the disease. You will always have villagers becoming sick and weak, and the medicine may not cure everyone."

Marius scowled. "We settled there so that we could harvest salt marsh hay for our livestock and easily travel and trade on the river Tiber. We have spent weeks building our homes. We cannot leave now!"

Marius motioned to Secundus, who quietly moved next to Scott. Lucy spied a silver glint and realized in horror that Secundus was holding a small knife against Scott's side. Scott appeared ready to argue further when he flinched at the touch of the blade and closed his mouth in a grim line.

Romi and Remi, if you're out there, this would be a good time to create a distraction! she thought desperately.

"For Apollo!" shouted Marius.

"For Apollo!" echoed the crowd.

Marius reached down and raised the ram's head, exposing its throat. The animal began bleating frantically and struggling in its bonds, and two men silently stepped forward to hold it down.

Oh no! thought Lucy. She struggled to maintain her composure, but one tear slid from the corner of her eye. *Romi, Remi, where are you?*

As if in reply, a wolf howled. With a collective gasp, the crowd turned to see the figures of two boys on a nearby ridge, a shaggy black wolf seated between them. *How was that, cousin?* Romi called out telepathically.

You do know how to make an entrance, Lucy answered. *Now what?*

136

A Doorway Through Time

The villagers watched, mesmerized, as a pack of wolves appeared from over the ridge and surrounded the boys. After a moment, Romi and Remi majestically descended from the hill and approached the altar, accompanied by the silent wolves. When they had come within a hundred feet of the crowd, the pack stopped and regarded the people menacingly. The villagers were shifting nervously in their places, many of the men standing with their hands on the knives hanging from their belts. Romi and Remi continued forward with the lone black wolf.

"Greetings, people of Latium," called Romi in perfectly accented Latin. "Lucia," he nodded to Lucy. "Scottus," he added with a smirk.

"You know this boy?" Marius demanded of Scott.

"Yes, he and his brother are Lucia's cousins," Scott explained.

"Cousins? Are they not children of Apollo?" asked Marius in surprise.

"No," interjected Romi. "Our father is Mars, the god of war. Our mother is Rhea Silvia, daughter of King Numitor, a princess of Alba Longa. I think our lineage is rather better than yours, peasant, and if you want to know more you should address me directly."

He certainly does have guts, thought Lucy, impressed.

"Why, you little..." began Marius, moving toward Romi.

The black wolf bared its teeth and snarled, and the

pack howled in support. The villagers whispered nervously, and Marius stopped abruptly. To Lucy's surprise, Crispus moved swiftly to Marius's side. "Lord Marius, you know that wolves are sacred to Mars. These boys must be his children if the wolves follow and obey them," Crispus said pleadingly. "Let us hear what they have to say."

"Well, young lord," said Marius sarcastically, "please tell us your names and explain why you're here."

"Gladly," returned Romi, ignoring Marius's tone. "My name is Romulus, and this is my brother, Remus. The wolves are not only our companions, they are our adopted family, and you will not hurt them. In return, the wolves will not hurt you—unless I tell them to."

Scott had quietly made his way back to Lucy and whispered in her ear, "Are their names really Romulus and Remus?"

"Maybe," she whispered back. "I don't really know. They've always been just Romi and Remi to me. Why?"

"Don't you remember the statue we saw that day in the Roman Forum?" asked Scott. "Romulus and Remus were the mythical twins who founded Rome. Or maybe not so mythical," his voice trailed off.

"I... I'll check the database," Lucy answered. "Database search. Romulus and Remus," she ordered quietly.

Her vision filled with pages of text. In the middle of one page was a picture of the familiar statue. "No wonder Romi wanted me to take a photo!" Lucy murmured to herself.

A Doorway Through Time

Romi, meanwhile, continued his narrative. "My uncle usurped the throne and had my brother and me put in a basket and thrown into the river Tiber. When we washed ashore, this she-wolf discovered us and suckled us like her own pups. We have lived with the wolves until now."

"Scott, you're right!" Lucy whispered urgently. "He's reciting the story of Romulus and Remus. It's a weird mix of fact and fiction. I mean, I guess the twins' full names must be Romulus and Remus, and my aunt's name really is Rhea Silvia!"

"And then there are the wolves," Scott added.

Romi paused, and Marius took the opportunity to break in. "So why exactly have you come to, ah, grace us with your presence?"

Romi raised an eyebrow. "Is it not obvious?"

Marius flushed in embarrassment, but remained silent. There was a buzz of noise as the villagers whispered amongst themselves.

Romi raised a hand to quiet the crowd, gave a superior smile, and shook his head. "You mortals cannot even see what is right before you. Tell them, brother."

Remi swallowed hard and adjusted his toga.

He's really nervous, Lucy realized. *But he's going to go through with it anyway.*

"Your village will always be sick and weak if you remain where you are," Remi began. "Romulus and I will lead you to a new place, where we will all build a village that will grow strong and prosper."

Romi stepped forward and addressed the crowd with authority. "Remus and I will live among you, and with the sons of Mars as your chieftains, and Domino Marius as your general, this tribe will thwart all attacks and strike others with deadly success. Let us show you the seven hills, where you will build a great city in my name and call it Rome."

Lucy clutched Scott's arm. "They're not going home with us!" she gasped.

"You are just boys," Marius objected. "How can you lead a tribe of men?"

"Can't you see the omens?" asked Romi with disdain. "The gods have chosen to intervene in your misery, sending Apollo's daughter, my cousin, to save you from the plague. Apollo's emissary told you that you must leave your settlement, and now Mars sends us to you as you prepare your sacrifice."

Romi strode toward the altar and drew his knife from his belt. "For Apollo and Mars!"

Lucy watched in stunned disbelief as Romi swiftly grabbed the ram by the horns, lifted its head, and slit its throat. As the ram's blood gushed out over the altar, the wolves began to howl in chorus. From high above, an eagle shrieked and wheeled in the sky, and the crowd gave a collective gasp.

I can't believe he did that! Lucy thought in horror.

A Doorway Through Time

Believe it, Lucy, Romi retorted. He addressed the crowd, "The gods are on our side. The wolves are on our side. Now will you stand by our side?" shouted Romi.

"It is a sign!" called out one swarthy shepherd.

"There are so many signs!" shouted another. "I will follow you, Romulus!"

"I will follow you, too," shouted yet another.

Lucy watched in amazement as the villagers all began shouting their support for Romulus.

What about Marius? she wondered. She scanned the crowd and saw him, apparently arguing with Secundus. Secundus finally turned his back on Marius and moved toward Romulus. Scott was watching the pair as well.

"Even Marius's lieutenant has deserted him," he observed in awe. "Your family has amazing charisma, Lucy."

"And I thought it was just me," Lucy joked weakly. "But Scott, what are we supposed to do now? Do we force the boys to go? It could be a little tough with the whole village trailing after them."

"Hey, you're a demi-god, too," Scott teased. "Call them over for a brief family conference."

Romi! Remi! Get over here! We need to talk! Lucy shouted telepathically.

Romi looked over in irritation and deliberately turned his back on her, but Remi tugged insistently on his brother's arm. Finally, Remi broke away from the crowd. Romi reluctantly followed him.

"Yes, cousin?" Romi asked impatiently.

"I've seen enough. More than enough. It's time to go home," Lucy declared. "You've got to do something—tell the people to get started on their feast or something—so that you can sneak away with us and head back to the time machine."

"We're not going back with you," Romi said calmly.

"What do you mean you're not going back with us?" Lucy demanded. "If this whole founding of Rome myth is so important to you, then show them where they need to build their city and come home with us."

"It's not a myth, Lucy. As you can see, it's happening right now," returned Romi.

"It is too a myth. You are not the son of a god."

"No, but a lot of it is the same," Remi broke in. "It feels like we've been preparing for this our whole lives. We know the language, we know how to dress, we know the stories, we know how everything should be. And for the first time, we feel like we belong somewhere."

· Remi reached down to pat the large female wolf by his side before continuing the narrative. "This is Genny, our adoptive wolf mother who has spent more time with us in the last couple of days than our own mother has spent with us all summer. We have a family in the wolves. We have never had a permanent home, but now we have a community here, with these people."

He sounds so mature, thought Lucy in surprise. Then

she remembered the final lines of the text she had read from her database page. She put a hand on Romi's arm. "What about the part of the story where Romulus wants to be the sole leader of the city, so he kills Remus? Did you think about that?" she asked.

Romi shook off her hand and answered, unflustered. "That's the story we knew before we went back in time. Who says we can't rewrite that chapter? It's not sacred, you know. What's the point of a time machine if you can't change history?"

Lucy stepped back in confusion. "I hadn't thought of it quite that way, but to save my father—"

"He has a point—" Scott admitted.

"I know what you think of me, Lucy," Romi said. "I didn't really like killing that ram, but I had to show the people that I was tough enough to be their leader. I would never murder my brother. He is going to be my second in command, my Secundus."

Lucy looked at Remi for confirmation. He shrugged and nodded.

"That's what I get for being born five minutes later. I'm used to it."

"And what exactly are we supposed to tell your parents?" asked Scott.

"When they finally notice we're gone, I expect they'll be happy," said Romi bitterly. "Now they won't have to worry about which relatives to dump us with."

143

He kinda does have a point, Lucy thought.

Remi broke in, his voice trembling a little. "Lucy, tell Mother—if she and Father really miss us, they should use your time machine to join us back here. But there's no way we want to go back to our old life."

Lucy and Scott exchanged helpless looks.

"Is there anything we can say to change your minds?" Lucy asked.

"Nope," replied Romi. "Besides, you'd have to change the minds of these fifty villagers while you're at it. They want us, and we want them. And now, if you'll excuse us, Remi and I have a celebration to attend. Thanks for the ride!"

With that, Romi blithely turned on his heel and left to rejoin the crowd. Remi, however, lingered behind.

"It'll be easy for you to slip away with so much going on," Remi said. "Sorry we were such pains in the neck this summer." He flung his arms around Lucy and gave her a tight hug. Lucy put her arms around her young cousin and squeezed him back. "Tell my mother that I love her," he whispered.

Before Lucy could reply, Remi broke away and ran back to his brother.

*"*I love you, too*, "* Lucy called, surprised to realize that it was true.

Lucy turned back to Scott. "So what do we do now?"

He shook his head in bemusement. "It's out of our

hands now. Maybe we really should send Rhea and Marcus back in time to fetch their kids themselves."

He looked around at the crowd that was milling about the twins. "We'd better get going before the crowd notices and gets insulted that we're skipping the feast."

Lucy sighed. "I guess you're right. Let them just think we flew back up to Olympus."

With a heavy heart, Lucy turned away from her cousins and headed up the hill, back to the time machine and home.

Chapter 13

Lucy and Scott picked their way carefully through the hillside scree, afraid lest a wayward step should start a small landslide. As the way got steeper, they moved without speaking, both focused on finding safe footholds. Suddenly, a savage shout rent the silence and a swiftly moving shadow leaped at Scott. Lucy turned to see Marius clinging to Scott's back. Scott lost his balance and fell to the ground, and the two men wrestled as they tumbled down the slope.

"Scott!" Lucy screeched. She reached under her toga for her dagger, then half-ran, half-slid down to join them. The men's swift descent had finally ended when they had landed, hard, on a rocky outcrop. Although Scott was the larger man, he had been taken completely unawares, and Marius had used this to his advantage. Marius still clung to Scott's back, one sinewy arm locked around Scott's throat. Scott was rolling and twisting, trying to dislodge his attacker, which had so far prevented Marius from striking a blow. There was a wild look in Marius's eyes and he was shouting in Latin between gasps for breath.

"You made me lose my command. You will pay with your lives!"

He's totally lost it, Lucy realized. "Not if I have anything to say about it!" she cried.

Marius, never loosening his grip, snarled back, "I don't believe you are Apollo's daughter. I'll take care of you next, and we'll see if your father has anything to say about it."

Lucy recoiled at the savagery in Marius's voice, and Scott made a gagging sound.

His face is starting to blue, Lucy realized. *I have to do something, fast.* Lucy jumped toward Marius, her dagger outstretched. Marius, however, was a seasoned warrior, and kicked out expertly at her right arm. With a cry of frustration, Lucy saw her blade fly from her hand and disappear down the hill. Marius chuckled and put renewed pressure on Scott's windpipe. In desperation, Lucy scooped up a large rock.

"Scott, roll onto your stomach and hold still!" she shouted.

With a mighty effort, Scott flipped over and lay on his belly. Lucy rushed over and slammed the stone against Marius's head. There was a sickening cracking sound, and Marius lay still. Scott curled into a fetal position and lay wheezing for several moments.

"Are you okay?" asked Lucy anxiously.

Scott raised himself up on his elbows, and Lucy helped him sit up.

"Yeah, thanks to you," he replied hoarsely. "Lucy, you're shaking like a leaf!"

"I can't believe I did that. Did I... kill him?" she asked with a quaver in her voice.

Scott slowly reached over and took Marius's limp wrist in his hand.

"He's got a strong pulse," he said. "The blood on his head is just seeping, not gushing out. He should be okay."

"I hope so," Lucy answered. "I mean, I know he was trying to kill you, but I'd hate to think I'd murdered anyone."

She blinked hard, trying to stop tears that were dangerously close to forming. "Could you just hold me for a minute?"

"Of course," Scott answered as he wrapped his arms around her.

Lucy sighed and leaned into his reassuring warmth. She could feel the tension in her body begin to ebb away. "Okay, we can keep going now," she murmured into his shoulder.

Scott gave her a final squeeze, and they turned to head back up the hill. They had been ascending for just a few minutes, Lucy leading the way, when there was a sudden rattle of gravel underfoot. Lucy turned just in time to see that Marius had somehow, impossibly, followed them. *He was just pretending to be unconscious,* she realized. She watched in shock as Marius jerked Scott's head back and delivered a punch to his bruised windpipe. Scott buckled over, winded as Marius followed the first blow with a swift kick to Scott's groin. Scott lay writhing on the ground in pain.

"No!" Lucy shouted, recovering from her shock. She launched herself at Marius, slamming into him with the full weight of her body. Marius was accustomed to this kind of hand-to-hand combat, however, and managed to keep his balance, just staggering slightly. Lucy kicked and punched wildly at him, but Marius quickly gained control and twisted one of her arms back so hard that Lucy's vision blurred with pain and she could hardly breathe. Marius used his free hand to grab and tear Lucy's toga.

"You... will... be... mine," he grunted with exertion.

Lucy forced herself to think through her pain. *What did I learn in self-defense class?* she thought frantically. *Oh yeah, go for the four vulnerable points...*

Lucy stomped hard on the instep of Marius's right foot. He howled and tightened his grip on her injured arm. Lucy stopped trying to push him away and instead balled her left hand into a fist. She used all her strength to punch him hard in the abdomen. Even Marius couldn't withstand this assault. The wind was knocked out of him, and he reeled backward, gasping for breath. But Marius took one step too many. He stepped off the edge of the cliff and

Judith Bourassa Joy

Lucy watched, frozen in horror, as Marius realized his mistake. Marius scrabbled frantically at the cliff as he tumbled down, but the rock was smooth and he could not find a good hold. Lucy rushed forward to help, but it was too late. Marius was gone. Scott rose painfully to his feet, and he and Lucy looked on in dismay as Marius fell for several seconds before landing on a jagged patch of rock. His head hit a large chunk of granite, and this time, the wound on his scalp split wide open, revealing the contents within. Lucy looked away, trying not to be sick. Scott gently turned her and led her a few steps away, so she could no longer see the horrible sight. She was beginning to hyperventilate.

"Shh," Scott whispered as he held her tight. "Slow, easy breaths. It's definitely over now."

Lucy shuddered. *This is a nightmare*, she thought in dismay. She closed her eyes and took several slow, deep breaths. Finally, she opened her eyes, then winced at the sight of the purple bruises already ringing Scott's neck. "You must really hurt," she whispered.

"I'll be okay," Scott replied, relieved to hear her speaking in normal tones. He started to brush the dirt from Lucy's toga, when she gently laid her hands on top of his.

"Don't bother," she said lightly. "It's a total loss."

The filthy garment hung in ribbons from her shoulders where Marius had torn it. Scott nodded. "Yeah, I guess you're right."

A Doorway Through Time

Lucy gave a rueful backward glance at her cousins and the crowd, now tiny figures in the far distance. "I guess we didn't need to worry they'd notice we'd gone and try to call us back. They forgot about us very quickly," she joked.

"Romi and Remi have always been good at keeping the spotlight on themselves," Scott returned. "For once, that's a useful quality."

Lucy was about to reply when she paused and tilted her head to the side, listening.

"What's up?" Scott inquired.

"Do you hear it?"

"Hear what?"

"That whimpering. I think it's coming from the other side of these bushes."

"We need to get going, Luce. Do you really think it's a good idea to find out what's making that noise?"

But Lucy was already off, pushing her way through the brush.

"I'll take that as a yes," Scott sighed, following her. He had caught up when Lucy stopped abruptly, causing Scott to bump into her.

"Sorry," he apologized, but Lucy paid no attention. Her focus was on a furry bundle lying prone on its side. The creature's sides were scratched, and blood flowed freely from its neck.

"Is it a..." Scott began.

"Wolf pup," Lucy finished. "Just look at the poor thing! He must have been trying to follow his mother, when something attacked him."

Scott observed the pup with a professional eye. "From the looks of those wounds, it was an animal with short, sharp claws. Maybe that eagle we saw just before the twins appeared?"

Lucy gasped. "I bet you're right."

She knelt down and extended a hand to the small, silver pup. The animal's eyelids flickered as it became aware of her presence. Its lips curled back, revealing a row of tiny, sharp teeth, and it uttered a low growl.

"Now Lucy, I know that's not a good idea."

"I'm not going to hurt you," Lucy murmured softly, ignoring Scott. She focused her thoughts on the animal. *I want to help you,* she tried telling the pup telepathically. The pup raised its head a few inches to regard Lucy. The wild look in its eyes slowly faded, and it stopped growling. Observing the change, Lucy reached out and tenderly stroked the pup's spine.

"You're something else," Scott said in grudging admiration.

Lucy flashed him a quick smile, then turned back to the small wolf. "How badly do you think he's hurt?"

Scott kneeled down near her. "The scratches on his side look crusted over, but those deep wounds on his neck are still bleeding. We've got to get that to stop. We need some sort of bandage."

He involuntarily glanced at Lucy's battered clothing.

"Oh," she said in sudden understanding. She looked down ruefully at her clothing. "My toga's already pretty much destroyed. I might as well finish it off." She tore a long strip of cloth from the cleanest section of her robe and held it out for the pup to see.

"This will make you feel better," she said to the pup in a low voice. He sniffed the cloth suspiciously, then lay his head back on the ground in apparent resignation. Lucy carefully wrapped the strip around the wounded neck as tightly as she dared, neatly tucking the end of the strip into the binding.

"Lucy, it looks good, but... aren't you forgetting something?" Scott asked.

"Like what?"

"Like how is he going to get that thing off once he's healed?"

"He's not going to take it off," she replied. "I'll do it. He's coming with us."

"But—"

"He won't survive on his own. He's just a baby who was loyally following his mom."

Lucy scooped the small wolf up from the ground. The puppy made a feeble attempt to snap at her, but Lucy gently gripped his muzzle and crooned softly to him, "You can't do that, little one." The pup struggled briefly, then relaxed in her arms. Lucy cradled him like a baby, lightly rubbing him behind the ears. She looked inquiringly at Scott. "What's the Latin word for 'loyal'?"

Scott thought for a moment. "Fidelis."

"Fidelis, that's what you are, a loyal, little boy," she said softly to the pup. "And that's what we'll call you. Fido for short."

Scott shook his head. "Unbelievable. And now you've got one of the oldest, cheesiest dog names in the book for him."

Lucy flashed a brilliant smile at Scott. "Well, we can't have people back home thinking I've got a wolf puppy— that would be illegal! Let them think he's just an unusually large... husky." She gave Scott an arch look. "And it is not a cheesy name." Lucy got a firmer grip on the puppy and began pushing her way out of the brush and back up the mountain. "You're going to love the 21st century, Fido," she told him in a reassuring voice. "You'll have all the food you could want, there are no nasty eagles to attack you, you'll have a whole house all to yourself..."

Scott gave a sigh and followed behind. He kept one hand on Lucy's back to help her balance on the slope with her unwieldy burden, and eventually they made it to the rocky outcrop that hid the entrance to the tunnel. Lucy peered nervously around the rock, and Fido whined.

"Man, it is so dark," she said with a shiver.

"Good thing we left the flashlights here," answered

A Doorway Through Time

Scott. "Thank you, Remi, wherever you are, for thinking of that. And since you've got, uh, Fido, I'll get the lights."

He reached down and groped behind the rock until he felt the pair of flashlights. He flicked one on, and the tunnel walls were suddenly revealed. Scott grinned at Lucy. "And then there was light. Ready, Luce?"

She nodded her assent, and they began the long journey down the tunnel toward the time machine, stopping frequently so that Lucy could rest her arms. Scott tried to take a turn carrying the young wolf, but Fido would have none of it, growling whenever Scott tried.

"You may have a one-man dog—I mean wolf—there," Scott said sadly.

"Don't worry, he'll get used to you," Lucy answered soothingly. "After all, I did," she added tartly.

"You got more than used to me," Scott retorted, drawing her to him for a long, fierce kiss.

Lucy gave a shiver and relaxed in his firm grip. For a moment, reality slipped away. A low growl drew them both back. "I think Fido wants us to break it up and get going."

"Too bad," Scott said, and pulled Lucy back to him for another long kiss.

The growling escalated until Scott finally released Lucy. Scott leaned down toward the small pup.

"It's fine to like Lucy best," he said firmly, "but you are not the alpha dog here. Got it?"

"He can't understand what you're saying," Lucy protested.

Scott stared hard at the pup. The wolf met his gaze for a few seconds, but then whimpered slightly and averted his eyes. "He may not understand my words, but he gets my meaning," Scott said with satisfaction. He peered ahead at the widened tunnel. "We're almost to the time machine, Lucy. I'll take Fido. Let's go!" To Lucy's surprise, this time Fido submitted and allowed Scott to carry him. They moved swiftly down the tunnel and into the cave, where the pod awaited them. Lucy turned off the flashlights. Their eyes, already accustomed now to the darkness, could see clearly in the glow from the time loop, the light rippling like liquid in a continuous current.

"Phew!" Lucy said in an undertone.

Scott turned to her in sympathy. "I know what you mean. I was kind of worried that maybe something might have happened to the time machine while we were gone."

Lucy reached out to pat the wolf pup in Scott's arms. "That's our ride home, Fido," she told him.

They hurried to the pod, and Lucy stepped inside. Immediately, her heart began pounding and she broke into a cold sweat. She stopped abruptly, breathing rapidly and shallowly.

"Lucy, is everything all right?" asked Scott in concern.

"I'm—I'm having some kind of panic attack, I think. I don't know why."

A Doorway Through Time

Scott gently set Fido down on the pilot's seat and turned back to Lucy. She still stood motionless next to the open door, pale and gasping for breath.

Scott carefully slid the door closed and put an arm around Lucy. "Come on, Luce," he urged her as he led her to the co-pilot's seat. "Sit down and put your head down on your knees. I don't want you fainting on me."

Lucy lowered herself into the chair, but sat stiffly upright, gripping the handles so tightly that her knuckles turned white. She gazed off into the distance, unseeing.

"Lucy?" Scott said. But Lucy was motionless, hearing a faint voice in her head.

The villa has been stormed. There's an armed guard trying to break into the lab. Hurry, Lucy!

The voice faded, and Lucy gave herself a little shake and took a deep breath. She gave Scott a small smile, but her eyes betrayed her uncertainty. "I know it's impossible, but I'd swear I heard a voice in my head."

"Whose?"

"Sayesha's. It was very faint, but she was trying to warn me about something. People were attacking the villa and trying to get to the lab. Impossible, right?" Lucy looked up at Scott, waiting for his reaction.

"It seems pretty unlikely that you could hear someone talking to you telepathically from 3,000 years in the future," he finally replied.

"I'm probably just going crazy," Lucy said. She bit her

lip and looked miserably at the ground.

"Well, stranger things have happened to us," Scott conceded. "And whatever may or may not be going on, I think we'd better get this thing fired up and head back home."

Lucy nodded in agreement. "You're right." She shakily fastened her seat belt. "You can give me Fido. I'll hold onto him for the ride."

"The worst is behind us, Luce," Scott said softly, enveloping her in a reassuring hug. "We'll just slip back into the time loop and be home in a few seconds."

"I know you're right, I don't know what came over me," Lucy agreed weakly.

Scott lightly kissed the back of her neck, and Lucy shivered with pleasure.

I've just got to keep my mind off my worries, she told herself. *We'll be back in the 21st century in no time.*

Scott gently picked up the wolf pup and deposited him into Lucy's waiting arms. He settled himself into the pilot's chair and pushed the Power button on. The dashboard display came to life, and Lucy gasped in surprise. "It looks different!" she exclaimed.

Scott leaned forward and studied the panel. "It is different—which is good. It either remembers, or senses, or both, that there is an active time loop in place." The spot where Lucy had entered the target destination was now replaced with a flashing message: 8.1.2065 AD < > 4.1.753 BC. Below that were two glowing green buttons labeled

Continue and Cancel.

"I guess Continue would be the one?" she mused.

"Must be," Scott agreed.

He reached over and pushed the Continue button. The date display changed to form a question:

Home? New Date In Loop?

"Okay, I need to set it to the date we actually wanted to travel to, so we can save your dad," said Scott, thinking out loud. "So I'll choose the second question."

He confidently touched the text on the screen. The dashboard display went blank, waiting for a new date. Carefully, Scott entered the date: 3.31.2064. He looked over at Lucy.

"Right?"

"Yup, that's the day before my dad's ship exploded," she agreed. Lucy gasped suddenly as she felt another wave of panic grip her. Fido, sensing her discomfort, whined uneasily. Lucy took short, deep breaths, trying to subdue her fear. *Cut it out, Lucy*, she told herself. *Everything's fine.*

Scott watched her silently in concern. After a few moments, Lucy took one more deep breath and visibly relaxed in her seat.

"Okay?" Scott asked gently.

"Ay, ay, captain."

Scott pushed the Continue button. They heard the click of the pod doors locking, and a faint rumble as the engine came to life. The pod began sliding backward.

"Why—?" Lucy began.

"Remember that the loop is behind us," Scott broke in, answering the unfinished question. "We came forward out of the loop, so we need to reverse direction to go back in. It's weird when there are no windows to see what's going on."

Lucy nodded and gripped the arms of the chair. *Why am I so nervous?* she wondered. *I hope I feel better once we slip back into the loop.*

After a few moments, the pod stopped moving, and Lucy and Scott experienced the stomach-lurching effect of zero gravity. Fido stirred, but did not wake.

"We're in the loop," Scott said reassuringly. "Soon we'll be out of here and on a plane, off to warn your dad."

Lucy forced a smile. "I know. I wish I knew why I feel scared. It's so ridiculous."

With a tremendous jolt, the pod landed—hard.

"That doesn't feel like last time," Scott said uneasily.

"It wasn't like last time. Something—or someone—stopped us. Look!" Lucy cried, pointing at the display. It was flashing a new message:

TRAVEL INTERRUPTED!
Current Date: 3.15.44 BC

"So that explains it," Lucy said savagely. A rush of anger flowed through her, drowning out her previously unnamed fear.

"Explains what?"

"My panic. I could feel this coming. This is no accident, Scott. Someone deliberately sabotaged our time loop."

"So now we're..." Scott began.

"Stuck. We're stuck here with no way to get home."

Chapter 14

Scott unbuckled himself from his seat and began pacing up and down the length of the pod. Lucy, on the other hand, remained in her seat, thoughtfully stroking Fido and considering the situation. *It's weird how calm I feel now. I feel better when I know what I'm up against.*

Scott finally broke the silence. "Okay, maybe it's not as bad as you think. It doesn't have to be a saboteur; it could just be a power glitch. Maybe there was a power failure back in the cave, and they're trying to reboot the time loop."

"Maybe," Lucy agreed. "But I don't think so. Somehow Sayesha found out about this, and her telepathy is so strong that her thoughts were carried to me in the time current. I can't hear her at all, now that the loop is off."

Scott's worried expression elicited Lucy's sympathy. "But let's suppose you're right for now, Scott. Whatever happens, we could use some food. Maybe by the time we've eaten and drunk something, the time loop will be back on."

A Doorway Through Time

But it won't, she thought privately.

Scott tried to smile. "Good idea, Lucy. Let's see what's in the storage bins."

Lucy unbuckled and placed the sleeping wolf pup carefully on the floor. She joined Scott and began hunting through the side cupboards with him. "Gross, there's just a lot of dried and canned stuff. Oh, here's some beef jerky. You want some?" she asked, offering a handful of beef strips to Scott.

He looked dubiously at the wrinkled, brown pile. "I'd have to be pretty hungry to eat that."

Lucy laughed. "Me, too. We'll call it Fido food, then."

After a concerted search, Lucy and Scott were rewarded with some mixed dried fruit, a jar of peanut butter, a box of crackers, and a few bottles of water. They sat cross-legged on the floor and enjoyed their picnic feast. Fido had roused himself at the smell of food and sat patiently nearby.

"Why doesn't he jump in and help himself?" Scott wondered.

"There's a pecking order at feeding time, I imagine," Lucy replied. "He must be waiting for the alpha dogs to finish—and that's us!" She tossed a strip of beef to the pup, who happily found a quiet spot to gnaw on his prize.

After Lucy and Scott finished every welcome morsel of their food, there was a moment of awkward silence.

Lucy looked expectantly at Scott. "So...?"

"So I guess I'll check on the time loop," he answered.

It's not going to be there, Lucy thought.

Scott slid open the pod door and stuck his head out. He slowly turned back to Lucy. "It's still not there."

"I don't think it will be back for quite a while," Lucy said quietly. "I just know it was terrorists, and I think it's going to take awhile to repair the time machine. But if Sayesha was able to warn me, maybe she warned Mom, too. I know she and Dr. Hartwick will work around the clock to get our time loop back up."

She was trying, but Scott didn't find her convincing. "Lucy?"

She smiled. "I don't know why I had a panic attack before and not now. But I feel like, somehow, things will work out. They always do seem to work out when we're together."

She stretched out her arms to Scott, and he pulled her close in a warm embrace. They held each other while Fido growled low in his throat.

"Now it's my turn to help you," she whispered in his ear. "You know what Romi and Remi would do if they were here?"

"Tell us to go out and explore?"

"Might as well!"

Scott stepped back and looked down at Fido. "What about him? He'll probably tear up the pod if we leave him alone. I'm pretty tired of carrying him around like a baby, though."

"Like a baby," Lucy slowly repeated. "That's it! Let's make a sling! I'll get a clean toga out of the cupboard and we can make a sling for him out of my old one." She took a few steps toward the cupboard, then stopped. "They do still wear togas in 44 BC, don't they?"

"Don't look at me. I'm not the expert. But maybe. Yeah, probably."

"Togas are what we've got, so togas are what we'll wear," Lucy decided.

After a series of trials and errors, they managed to construct a workable baby sling for Fido.

"You want to go first, or should I?" asked Scott.

"Why don't you carry him up the tunnel," Lucy answered. Once we're out in the open, I'll take him. If we run across any natives, they'll probably expect to see the woman carrying the baby."

"Sounds like a plan," Scott agreed.

They headed out of the pod, and after one last, longing look at the place where the time loop should have been, they switched on their flashlights and began hiking up and out of the mountain. After a long, wearisome journey, Scott and Lucy finally emerged, blinking, into the light. An orange glow suffused the horizon, and the sun was just emerging, a pulsing, golden globe.

"Dawn," Lucy breathed. "It's so beautiful! But—" She paused in confusion. "Did we really come out in the same place?"

They were once again standing on the rocky outcrop, looking down into the valley toward the Tiber River. The scene before them, however, looked nothing like the landscape they had left only hours earlier. The fields of sheep and groves of olive trees were gone. In their place were scores of neatly arranged stone buildings, each with its own small paddock for livestock. A pale road carved a route through the valley. Gravel tracks led toward the river, where a variety of boats plied the waters. Most astonishing of all was the city that now straddled the tamed river. Lucy and Scott gaped at the vast assortment of buildings clustered in the distance, gleaming in the rays of the rising sun.

Lucy swallowed hard. "A lot happened in the last few centuries."

"I'll say," Scott agreed. "Romi and Remi started something pretty amazing."

Lucy gripped Scott's hand in excitement. "The Roman Forum—the ruins we saw in the 21st century—we're going to see it whole! We're going to see it the way Julius Caesar did!"

Scott looked down at her face, shining with excitement, and chuckled. "You're right! It's going to be awesome! Are you ready for our next adventure?"

Lucy glanced down at the road. It was nearly empty, except for a few peasants trudging along beside their laden oxen, wending their way to Rome.

"Let me just tuck the baby in, so nobody asks any questions."

She tightened the sling and tucked loose ends of the cloth lightly over Fido's face. He was sound asleep, snoring gently. "Ready."

They continued to hold hands, helping one another down the slope. At last, they came to the bottom of the mountain. Lucy tightened the sling, and she and Scott jumped over a narrow ditch and up onto the wide, paved road.

"Just look at this," Scott marveled. "The pavers are perfectly square, and there are hardly any seams."

"Mm-hmm," Lucy agreed absently. "Since it leads to Rome, I'm thinking it must be that famous road we saw before—the Appian Way?"

"Yeah. That's pretty incredible, too. How many modern roads do you think could last for centuries?"

"Ummm, none. C'mon Scott," she said, tugging on his sleeve. "The Appian Way leads straight to the Forum. Now *that's* going to be impressive."

They traveled swiftly, overtaking the peasants they had seen from the hillside, who nodded pleasantly as they passed. More locals joined them on the road as they neared the city, some on foot, some with horse or oxen drawn wagons, others on horseback or mule. Most were carrying goods to sell—mainly fruits and vegetables. Many carts had livestock tied behind, calmly following along, switching their tails, blissfully unaware that they would soon be bound for some Roman housewife's table.

"The road's really filling up," Lucy said in a low voice. "Do you think it's market day?"

"Must be," Scott concurred. "That's good, though. We can blend in better if there's a big crowd."

Trying not to stare at the people, Lucy distracted herself by studying the many tall stone monuments that lined the road. She was supporting Fido in the sling with one hand and holding Scott's hand with the other. She squeezed his hand now. "What do you think all these stone things are along the road?" she asked.

Scott paused and squinted at the inscription on the nearest monolith. "Uh, looks like they're family tombs."

"Huh," Lucy said, unimpressed. "Why didn't we see those when we visited Rome before?"

"They may have been in ruins, or maybe the stones got reused for other buildings," Scott replied. "But look straight ahead—we're near the city!"

Lucy struggled to take in the sight before her. Homes and shops, constructed of clay and stone, nestled against one another, making the road seem narrower. As they passed into the city limits, a stone piazza opened up, but it was jammed full of wooden stalls with local farmers and vendors hawking their wares. The noise of the crowd, the cries of the sellers, and the bleating, lowing, and clucking of the various animals was deafening. The smell of sweat, animals, and food mingled in the air. Lucy and Scott stood out in their togas; most of the people wore simple tunics.

"Why are there so few people in togas?" Lucy asked.

Scott looked around in surprise. "I hadn't noticed. But you're right." He paused to consider. "Maybe people rich enough to wear togas are rich enough to send their servants or slaves to the market."

"And I don't think farmers would wear togas," Lucy reasoned. "It wouldn't be too practical."

"Lady, gentleman," one of the fruit vendors interrupted them. "See my beautiful limes? They are the best in Rome! Try one, and you will want to buy a dozen!"

"Fresh meat!" shouted another vendor to Scott. "No worms in my lambs! Would you like to buy one?"

"No, thank you," Lucy answered nervously.

Scott ignored the sellers and put an arm around Lucy. "C'mon, let's get out of here," he said in an undertone as he pushed his way through the crowd.

They found a series of back streets, and they narrowly avoided an unwelcome, dirty shower as a pitcher was emptied through an upstairs window. There was a sour smell of urine and decay, and Lucy was glad when they emerged onto a wider avenue. Ahead of them was a large green space, a welcome sight in the crowded city. A long building was set in the park-like area. It was low, but still imposing, lined with beautifully fluted columns. Intricate carvings decorated the roofline, and an elaborate garden

169

in the front was adorned with exquisite statuary. The scent of roses filled the air.

"This is a pretty impressive building," Scott remarked. "It looks kind of familiar."

Fido was awake and beginning to squirm, so Lucy removed him from the sling and set him down. He immediately went toward the garden and relieved himself on a flowering bush.

"No, Fido! Come back!" Lucy called out.

She and Scott chased after the pup, but Fido was well rested and in no mood to be caught. He dashed ahead and disappeared in the nearest bed of roses.

"Here, Fido!" Lucy called softly, getting down on her hands and knees.

Scott stooped over and began pacing along the edge of the garden, peering through the roses and shouting Fido's name. Without warning, a toga-clad man appeared with sword in hand. He grabbed Scott's shoulder and raised the sharp edge of his sword to strike. Lucy looked over just in time. "Wait!" she shouted. "We are strangers! What have we done?"

The warrior paused and looked at Lucy. Her blue eyes shone fiercely, and her red hair gleamed in the sunlight. She was tall and regal in her toga, and for a brief moment, the man thought he was beholding a goddess. He silently considered Lucy, then turned back to Scott. "Stand up very slowly and put your hands up in the air," the warrior said in a menacing voice.

Scott slowly rose and raised his hands. The man glared at him and shook his head warningly at Lucy, who longed to race to Scott's side.

"I should have killed you," the soldier said to Scott. "You are on sacred territory. No man may enter here, under pain of death."

"We are foreigners in the city, sir, and did not know we should not come here," Lucy said winningly—in her best Latin. "Please forgive us and let us go. We promise never to trouble you again."

The soldier looked puzzled. "That is a very strange accent you have, indeed. Where are you from?"

"We are Thracian, lord," Scott broke in humbly, remembering Crispus's guess.

The soldier shook his head. "You should know better," he said with a growl. "You should recognize the House of the Vestal Virgins."

"We beg your pardon," Scott said, his head bowed. "We have no buildings as grand as this where we come from. We are simple folk. We will be more careful. We were chasing our puppy, who escaped from us."

The warrior released his hold on Scott, but he kept his sword at the ready. His expression was puzzled. "You are well-dressed for simple folk," he said grudgingly. "And where is this puppy you're searching for? I don't hear or see anything."

Fido, get over here! Lucy shouted telepathically. She tried picturing strips of beef jerky in her mind.

"That's exactly it," Lucy said with a hint of irritation. "We can't see him, either. That's why we're searching for him."

Before the warrior could reply, there was a soft whine, and a long snout pushed its way between two red rose bushes.

"Good boy, good Fido," Lucy whispered as she slowly coaxed the puppy.

Fido took one step back, but Lucy pounced and grabbed him by the scruff of the neck. Squirming and protesting all the while, he was thrust into the sling. The soldier burst out laughing. "Begone, and never darken this place with your shadow again. Next time, there will be no warning—only pain."

"Thank you, sir," Scott said gratefully as Lucy hastily backtracked.

They moved to the far side of the street, which ran parallel to the House of the Vestals, looking straight ahead and walking rapidly. After they had passed the house, a circular building came into view.

Lucy stopped suddenly and turned toward the building. "The Temple," she said aloud to herself.

"Lucy, why are you stopping?" Scott demanded. "We're going to aggravate that soldier if you keep it up."

Lucy glanced at the figure of the soldier, pacing along

the length of the house, on patrol, but she held her ground. "Scott, the House and Temple of the Vestal Virgins are major monuments that no one from our century has seen whole. I need some pictures."

Lucy clutched Fido tightly to her chest to hold him still and used her contacts to capture several images. As she snapped the photos, she saw robed figures hurrying along the marble portico, behind the line of columns. A woman bearing a torch emerged, followed by a phalanx of other women.

"Those must be the priestesses on their way to re-light the fires in the temple," she said softly. "Maybe that would have been me, if I had lived in this time."

"It was probably a better life than most women had," Scott remarked.

"I wouldn't like being told what to do all day long and never getting to leave the temple," Lucy returned.

Scott looked fondly at her and smiled. "No, you wouldn't. You're lucky to have been born in the 21st century."

"You, too," Lucy retorted. "I think you like modern conveniences."

"I do. Although remember, the Romans were pretty advanced. They actually had plumbing and baths."

"I think they could stand to take a few more baths," Lucy said drily. "Although they do seem cleaner than Marius and company."

They paused to observe the temple silently for a few

more moments. Finally, Lucy turned to Scott. "If we've made it to the Temple of the Vestal Virgins, then we're almost to the main forum. Let's find out how that's changed, too!"

Fido was whining and twisting in the sling, anxious to get down again. Lucy grimaced. "He's squirming like crazy—I won't be able to hold him much longer."

"If Fido won't be carried anymore, then we'd better make him a leash," Scott said.

"How can we put a leash on him when he's got that wound on his neck?"

Scott considered, "We can make a harness and leash from the sling. Let's go sit over there." He nodded at a large, ornate fountain in the center of the street. "And I'll give it a try."

They seated themselves on the edge of the fountain, and while Lucy kept a firm hold on Fido, Scott tore the sling into long strips of cloth. He braided the pieces and knotted sections. In a matter of minutes, he had tied together two woven loops, which he fitted over Fido's shoulders and around his belly. Fido squirmed and complained with little grunts and whines, but the harness went on, nonetheless.

"Not bad," Scott murmured to himself. "I just need to tighten up the main loop a little."

"You're really good," Lucy commented admiringly.

"All that knot-tying in Boy Scouts was pretty useful,"

he replied with a smile. "The harness was the hard part. The leash will be easy."

A few minutes later, a leash was woven and tied to the harness. Lucy set Fido down with a sigh of relief, and he immediately tried to dash off. The look of surprise on his face when he found himself suddenly halted by his connection to Lucy made her laugh out loud. "Sorry, little wolf, but you have to act like a big dog now," she told him. "Okay, Scott, let's keep going!"

"Lucy, check out this fountain we were sitting on. Do you see what I see?"

Lucy looked up, realizing she had thought of the fountain as a bench—not as a piece of art. Her eyes traveled up from the carved base, to the spouting water, to the statue at the top. It depicted a large wolf, flanked by two boys. Lucy stared at the faces of the boys. "It's Romi and Remi," she breathed.

"That means they really did alter history. They're no longer babies under the belly of the wolf. They're standing next to their wolf mother like they were when we left them. They're memorialized for all time."

"I wish they could see this," Lucy said in wonder. "Maybe, somehow, we'll see them again, and they can see my pictures."

She took more photos, then blinked twice to return to normal vision. "Whew, that was spooky." She gave herself a little shake. "Let's check out that giant building up ahead."

Behind the fountain rose a rectangular marble structure, imposing in scale. High, wide steps led to a portico rimmed with columns. Guards could be seen patrolling the perimeter. A pair of enormous wooden doors stood shuttered in front, and carved above the doors were the words, DOMUS REX RGIS.

"House of the Kings," Lucy translated.

"The Regia!" Scott cried. "I remember the guidebook said it would have been here but that nothing remains of it in our century."

"So this would be Caesar's house!" Lucy exclaimed. "Maybe we'll see Caesar himself!"

Scott grinned at her enthusiasm. "Maybe. But I don't think those guards would let us get too close. C'mon, let's go around it. If I remember correctly, the main forum should stand behind here."

As they skirted their way around the Regia, the busy street became more crowded, and this time, not just with people on their way to buy or sell goods. Heavy-laden wagons of stone and sand, pulled by patient teams of oxen, were trundling along, sending pedestrians scurrying to the edges of the road. The noise was deafening, an overwhelming jumble of iron wheels creaking and clattering, animals bleating and lowing, and people shouting.

"Ugh," said Lucy as she and Scott were forced to press up against a crowd of men carrying baskets of fish, to avoid being trampled by the wide hooves of the plodding oxen. "Where are they going?"

"Constructing more buildings, I guess," Scott answered in a low voice. He put a finger to his lips. "Now keep your voice down, so more people don't ask about our weird accents."

"Right," Lucy whispered back.

They pushed forward with the rest of the crowd until they reached the entrance of the forum. There they paused, struck by the space ahead of them.

"I could never imagine how it would really be," Lucy said in awe.

The forum was an enormous, open space. The floor was lined with limestone pavers. Buildings and temples lined the perimeter. Scott seemed enraptured by the scene.

"There's the Basilica Aemilia," he said, pointing at an imposing building at the side of the forum.

Lucy recognized it, too, from the arches along the first floor. They were ten barrel-vaulted arches, flanked by columns. The shopkeepers inside appeared to be doing a brisk business, as there was a steady flow of people in and out. Two more floors were constructed above, and although the basilica was massive in scale, it was so well-proportioned that it appeared graceful and welcoming.

"Right, and across from that is the Temple of Castor and Pollux," Lucy added, gesturing at the enormous, house-like building, fronted by ornate columns.

"So that would be the Basilica Julia they're working

177

on next door to the temple," Scott said.

"And the temples of Saturn and Concord are there on the far end," Lucy finished. "I can't wait to explore them all!"

They stood in silent admiration, taking in the wealth of marble and limestone, the columns, arches and statuary. They marveled at the nonchalance of the busy Roman people, who casually went about their business in the midst of all this grandeur. A man walked by them, leaving the Forum with a tray of steaming meat pies. Fido began straining at his leash and whining.

"I know you must be hungry, but we have more to do first," Lucy told him. "Where to, Scott?"

"We're right next to the Basilica Aemilia—let's check that out."

They started toward the basilica arm in arm, chatting happily in low tones. Lucy held the leash loosely while Fido continued to whimper and lag behind. Suddenly, the wolf pup jerked hard, pulling the leash from Lucy's hand. She whirled around to see the puppy chasing after the man with the meat pies. "Not again," she moaned.

There was a sudden influx of people into the Forum, and although the pup slipped easily between them, Lucy and Scott found it difficult to make their way. They emerged from the Forum just in time to see Fido a few feet ahead, chasing after the meat, oblivious to a wagon bearing down on him.

"Fido, no!" Scott shouted.

Look out, Fido, Lucy shouted telepathically. *Get out of the way!*

To Lucy's astonishment, a hooded man darted out from the side of the road, grabbing the pup just before the wagon's iron wheels could crush him. The man turned and stared at Lucy. She felt a painful twinge in her forehead and heard a deep voice in her head. *Who are you? I know of no Akwatair with hair like yours.*

Lucy grabbed Scott's arm and leaned heavily against him. "That man," she began.

"I know. He saved Fido!" Scott replied.

"It's more than that, Scott. He's—" she gulped— "an alien. He's an Akwatair."

Chapter 15

The Akwatair had very long legs, so he was by their side in three bounding strides. Fido whined and squirmed in his arms, but the alien seemed not to notice. Instead, he peered into Lucy's face and stepped back in astonishment. "You are human!" he exclaimed in a low voice.

Yes, but I have visited your planet, Tairran, Lucy answered.

The alien raised one odd-looking eyebrow and looked skeptically at her. *That is impossible!* he said angrily. *Humans haven't even developed primitive engines, much less spaceships.*

It's not impossible, Lucy informed him impatiently. *We're from the future.*

From the future? the alien repeated dubiously. *How can that be? How far in the future?*

More than 2,000 years, Lucy answered. She held out her arms. *Thank you for saving my puppy—but can I have him back now?*

The Akwatair looked down in surprise at Fido, who

was now gripping the alien's arm with his tiny jaws. *I'd forgotten I was holding him*, he replied. *You have taken me by surprise.*

He handed the pup to Lucy, who set Fido on the ground and wrapped the leash firmly around her hand.

Why doesn't he say anything? the Akwatair asked abruptly, nodding his head at Scott. *Is he... mentally deficient?*

Lucy roared with laughter, while Scott, aware they were talking about him, looked vaguely uncomfortable.

My friend Scott is not a true telepath, Lucy explained. *He could communicate a little on Tairran when he was surrounded by your people, but he can't do it back here on Earth.*

"Interesting," murmured the alien aloud in Latin. He stood silently stroking his chin with his long fingers.

Scott and Lucy were transfixed by the sight of the alien's finger webbing, which extended almost up to his knuckles. The Akwatair suddenly became aware of their gaze and smiled briefly. "One of the signs of my people," he said. "That is why they have named me and my comrades the Ranaegens—the Frog-people. It's more accurate than they realize!" He made a small, elegant bow. "Ædifex Ranaegens, that is my name here. And you are—?"

"I am Lucy Starrett, and this is Scott Davenport." She attempted a curtsey, and Scott bowed.

Ædifex looked amused. "Not exactly Latin names. Do

you come from a different land as well as a different time?"

Lucy nodded.

"Well, Lucy and Scott, may I invite you to my home and offer you some food and drink? There is much I would like to ask you."

"That sounds good," Scott said, finally joining in the conversation. "I'm starving."

"Yes, thank you," added Lucy. "Where do you live?"

"In the apartment across the street. Over the tailor's shop. Come with me."

Ædifex led them across the street to a narrow doorway nearly hidden between two shops. As Scott closed the heavy wooden door behind them, the noise from the street was largely muffled. Lucy breathed a sigh of relief.

I didn't realize how noisy it was out there, she thought.

You get used to it, Ædifex reassured her telepathically.

Just like I'll get used to someone hearing my thoughts, she retorted good-naturedly.

Ædifex laughed out loud and continued up the stairs. He reached into a pouch slung from his leather belt and produced an iron key, which he used to unlock the door to his apartment. "Welcome to my home," he said aloud for Scott's benefit.

They stepped into a living area, and Lucy looked around with approval. Geometric mosaic borders surrounded the perimeter of the room. A small stone fountain, decorated with carved lilies and lily pads, stood in one corner. A grinning frog topped the fountain, and the sound of water splashing from its wide mouth rendered any lingering sounds from the street nearly inaudible. A thick carpet covered the center of the floor, and a number of large, colorful pillows lay stacked on one edge of the rug. A chaise longue was placed along one wall with a low, square table in front of it. A bowl of green grapes and a pitcher of water sat invitingly on the table.

"Please make yourselves comfortable," Ædifex told Lucy and Scott. "I will get some wine and bread, and then we will talk."

Once Ædifex left the room, Lucy picked up Fido and let him drink from the fountain.

"Drink fast," Scott told the wolf pup. "Ædifex might not like you in his fountain."

When Fido had consumed his fill, Lucy set him down on the floor, where he promptly stretched out on the cool tiles and closed his eyes. "He's still such a baby," Lucy said fondly. "He sleeps a lot."

"He did just have a lot of excitement," commented Scott. He reached for Lucy's hand and gently pulled her towards the chaise. They seated themselves on the soft cushion, and Scott put one arm around her. She sighed and happily leaned against him. "Kind of different to have a fountain in your living room," she remarked.

"Yup," Scott agreed. "But we know Akwatairs are pretty much amphibians, so he must use it to stay hydrated at home."

Lucy leaned forward to pluck a grape from the bowl. She took a bite and grimaced. "Ugh, I forgot they wouldn't have developed seedless grapes yet."

"Just swallow the seeds. You swallowed a lot worse when we were the guests of Akwatairs," Scott said with a grin.

Lucy had a brief, unpleasant memory of eating leech soup on Tairran.

"Thanks a lot," she grumbled, "I'd blocked that from my memory."

"Think about this instead, then," said Scott. "Can't you just picture Cleopatra lying on this couch?"

"Definitely," she agreed, "with one slave fanning her with a palm leaf and another one dropping grapes into her mouth." Lucy lay back dramatically on the chaise longue, draping her legs over Scott. "Go ahead, Scott, drop a grape in my mouth!"

Ædifex was standing still in the doorway holding a large silver tray. The tray held a painted terra-cotta jug, three metal goblets, a round loaf of bread, a hunk of cheese, and a small bone. His round, golden eyes were wide with surprise. "Did I hear the name Cleopatra?" he asked excitedly. "Do you know the queen? She is here in Rome, you know, visiting Julius Caesar."

Lucy scrambled to swing her legs around and sit up.

"No way!" Scott exclaimed.

184

"No, we don't know her, we were just saying that your beautiful couch looked worthy of the queen," Lucy explained in Latin. "I was just, uh, acting the part."

Fido's eyelids fluttered, and he sat up, sniffing the air with his pointed nose.

"Fido smells the bone!" Lucy exclaimed. "May I give it to him?"

Ædifex handed her the bone, but his thoughts were clearly elsewhere. "What language were you speaking before?" he asked.

"English," Lucy answered. She noticed the confusion in his eyes. "Anglo-Saxon?" she tried. "Celtic?"

"Oh, the island barbarians in the north," Ædifex exclaimed. "I have heard of them. Surely Julius Caesar will soon make them part of the Roman Empire?"

"Hardly," Lucy answered, laughing. "But that's another story. Maybe you could tell us what you Akwatairs are doing here?"

"If you promise to tell me about yourselves," Ædifex returned.

"Of course!" she replied.

"But refreshments first," he said as he placed the tray of food and drinks on the table. He dragged one of the pillows over and carefully seated himself on the cushion. Finally, he pulled the stopper from the jug.

"Actually, I'll just drink water, thanks," Lucy broke in.

"Uh, me, too," added Scott.

185

Judith Bourassa Joy

A look of annoyance crossed Ædifex's face, but it quickly cleared. "Things must be very different in the future," he remarked drily. "But as you wish."

Ædifex filled his own goblet with wine while Scott poured water into his and Lucy's glasses. "A toast to my visitors from the future, Lucy Starrett and Scott Davenport," Ædifex said, raising his goblet.

Lucy and Scott quickly picked up their glasses.

"Ave," said Ædifex, clinking his goblet against theirs.

"Ave," Lucy and Scott replied politely.

Ædifex took a long drought of wine and wiped his mouth with the back of his tanned, but slightly greenish, arm. "Let me think about how to begin. My people first noticed your planet a few centuries before this one—on one of our exploratory missions. We were intrigued by what we found: sentient creatures with great potential for intellectual growth, much like early Akwatairs. Eons ago, our civilization was visited by aliens from a distant planet who helped us make significant technological gains. These aliens asked only that we return the favor someday—when we were able. With that in mind, we surveyed Earth to determine how we could best assist your nascent race."

"Pay it forward," Scott murmured softly in English.

"What did you decide to do?" Lucy asked.

Scott was very quiet, looking off in the distance.

"I think Scott can guess," Ædifex said shrewdly.

186

A Doorway Through Time

Scott blinked and turned toward Ædifex. "It must have something to do with all the buildings the Romans are famous for—like their roads and colosseums."

Ædifex slapped his knee in delight. "That's it exactly!" he exclaimed. "We turned the Romans into masters of civil engineering. We began by teaching them the secrets of road building, which enabled them to link their ever-expanding conquests and develop efficient trade routes." He swiveled his bulging eyes in Lucy's direction. "And can you guess what we taught the Romans next?"

Lucy made a tentative probe of Ædifex's mind, but he anticipated her attempt and blocked her efforts.

Lucy grinned. "Okay then, no cheating. Give me a second..." She looked over at the fountain. *Of course! It must have to do with water!*

"I'm guessing you wanted to make life nicer for the Akwatairs here, so maybe you built the famous Roman bath houses? Or the aqueducts?"

"Yes and yes!" Ædifex delightedly confirmed. "We taught the Romans to bring water to their growing, thirsty cities. Once their people had access to clean, safe water, we showed them the finer things in life: public baths with hot and cold water—and indoor plumbing. Let me assure you, it made life on Earth much easier for Akwatairs, once we knew we could stay safely hydrated all day long."

"You did an incredible job," Lucy told him. "3,000 years later, those roads and aqueducts are still holding up pretty well. In fact, even though we pipe our water underground now, some of your aqueducts are still being used as bridges. Roman buildings were harder hit over the years by invading armies, but there's still plenty of amazing stuff to see, like the Pantheon or the Colosseum in Rome."

Ædifex grinned broadly. "I am so pleased to hear that you still respect the Romans' achievements even thousands of years in the future. And if you want to give them all the credit, so be it. We taught them the skills, but they did the work."

"But if the Romans know what they're doing now, then why are you still here?" asked Lucy.

Ædifex cleared his throat, and his tanned face flushed turquoise. *Oh my gosh, he's blushing,* Lucy realized with surprise.

"There are few, maybe fifty, of us left," Ædifex finally choked out. "We have grown very fond of Earth and its people—certain people, in particular. I am, in fact, engaged to be married to a most beautiful and intelligent Roman woman next month, my precious Agrippina. My fellow Akwatairs on Earth have all intermarried as well."

"Will that—uh, work?" Lucy asked awkwardly.

"Lucy!" Scott interrupted in shock.

Ædifex turned a deep shade of teal. "My friends have become the proud parents of many half-breed children, if that's what you mean."

"Scott, do you realize what that means?" Lucy said

excitedly in English. "Maybe you and I—or even most people on Earth in the future—have a little Akwatair in us!"

"That would explain why it was relatively easy for us to communicate with them," Scott returned thoughtfully.

"Latin, please? Or telepathy?" Ædifex requested.

"Sorry Ædifex," Lucy apologized in Latin. "I was just wondering if maybe lots of humans in the future are descended from Akwatairs."

Ædifex inclined his head in a small bow. "It seems very possible. I have no desire to return to Tairran, and neither do my compatriots. But I have told you a great deal about myself and the role of Akwatairs on Earth. Would you please return the favor by telling me your story?"

Lucy launched into a retelling of her adventures, beginning with her father's death and her mother's disappearance, then continuing on with the story of her trip through the wormhole and discovery of the planet Tairran. Ædifex winced when she described how the Akwatairs had been enslaved by their government, but he remained silent. Lucy paused for a sip of water, and Scott took up the thread of the narrative. "We found Lucy's mom and her crew being held captive—the government wanted to use their DNA to strengthen the Akwatair gene pool and planned to kill all the humans afterward," Scott explained. "For some reason, Lucy looked just like one of their ancient goddesses, OppelLo, so we used that to our advantage."

189

Ædifex could no longer contain himself. "OppelLo!" he cried. "Do you not see where that came from?"

"What do you mean?" asked Lucy with interest.

"Their fire goddess, OppelLo—that must be derived from the Roman god of the sun, Apollo, who in turn was adopted from the Greek god of the same name." Ædifex laughed with delight. "Oh, it's marvelous how civilizations adapt and grow from one another. Indeed, my predecessors on Earth were so enamored of the culture here that I did hear they had documented Roman mythology and their pantheon of gods."

"It must have been pretty persuasive writing," Scott said under his breath.

"Wow, I can't believe we never made that connection," Lucy said, shaking her head in amazement.

"I have interrupted you. I apologize. Please continue," implored Ædifex graciously.

And so Lucy continued her monologue, with asides from Scott, telling Ædifex about the civil revolt she had inspired and their thrilling escape from the planet, with all the human captives safely spirited away. She told Ædifex about their latest adventures and how Lucy's hope of going back in time to save her father had been twice thwarted: first by Romi and Remi, who stayed behind to oversee the founding of Rome, then by the rupture in the time loop. "Now we're here with a broken time machine and no way to get home," Lucy concluded.

A Doorway Through Time

"That is an amazing story, Lucy OppelLo," Ædifex said solemnly. "I can see that you and Scott are brave, honorable people, with important parts to play in your own history and in the history of my people. I will help you in your quest to save your father."

Before Lucy could respond, she became aware of a rumbling outside the building. Fido had stopped chewing his bone and was pacing nervously around the room, whining. Lucy sniffed the air. "Something's burning!" she cried.

"There must be trouble outside," said Ædifex nervously. "Come, let us see."

Lucy grabbed hold of Fido's leash, and they all rushed out of the apartment and into the street. A wave of heat engulfed them, and Lucy saw that the tailor's shop next door was burning. They were overwhelmed by a cacophony of men and women screaming, babies crying, and animals lowing and whinnying in fear. Fido pulled hard on the leash, making strange noises that were a mix of a bark and a howl.

"What's going on?" Scott shouted in Ædifex's ear. "This seems like an overreaction for a small fire."

"It is more than that!" Ædifex shouted back. "The whole city is in an uproar. This fire was set—don't you see the looting?"

Lucy looked around and saw with surprise that while most people were pushing one another and running in the street without clear purpose, some men were breaking down doors of the local shops and stealing whatever they could. A whip cracked, and Lucy turned to see a litter being forced down the street, carried by four burly, dark men with straight black hair. The men were richly attired in linen garments and gold jewelry. Two men went before them, lashing out with whips to scatter the crowd and clear a path. Lucy, Scott and Ædifex pressed themselves against the wall of the apartment building to make way for them. Lucy strained to see who was being carried. A woman with long hair and a horsy, dark-skinned face, dressed in an elaborate robe and heavy gold jewelry, lay on the litter, weeping.

"Queen Cleopatra!" Ædifex exclaimed worriedly. He closed his eyes.

He's scanning the minds in the crowd, Lucy realized.

Ædifex suddenly opened his eyes wide in alarm and clutched Lucy's and Scott's arms. "It is Julius Caesar!" he shouted in shock. "He has been assassinated by members of the Senate, including his best friend, Brutus!"

"Beware the Ides of March," Scott said suddenly. "Remember your high school Shakespeare?"

"March 15, the date of Caesar's murder!" Lucy recalled. "But I never knew the year Caesar was assassinated."

"We must get out of here," Ædifex said urgently. "My home will soon be engulfed by these flames. Follow me!"

He took off at a run down the street, turning sharply into a narrow alleyway.

"Where are we going?" Lucy panted as she and Scott struggled to keep up with Ædifex's oversized strides.

"To the only safe place at the moment," Ædifex replied grimly.

To Lucy's surprise, he leaned over a circular stone on the side of the street and quickly pried it out of the road. A horrendous odor wafted from below, and Lucy recoiled in disgust.

"We must go into the sewer," said Ædifex firmly. "Now."

Chapter 16

"Isn't there anyplace else we could go?" Lucy cried in horror.

"We are in the heart of the city, and I know of no other way to avoid the dangers from both the mob and the fire. Perhaps you have a better suggestion?"

Lucy could hear the cries of panicked people and animals drawing nearer. Black smoke was obscuring the sky and making it hard to breathe.

"No, I don't," she admitted. "Although I wouldn't call your way easy."

"Enough talking. Come on!" shouted Ædifex. He sat on the edge of the hole and leaped into the blackness. There was a splash as he landed.

"Ewww," said Lucy faintly. "I think I'm going to puke."

Scott briefly flashed a grin at her. "I know what you mean, but we'll just have to deal. Make sure you breathe through your mouth, and you'll be okay. I'll go first and help you down slowly, so you don't splash so much."

"All right," said Lucy heavily. "Don't forget you'll

have to help Fido down, too."

Fido was whining and straining on his leash, and Lucy nearly slipped on the pavement, trying to hold him in place.

"Calm down, Fido!" she said impatiently. "We're trying to keep you safe."

Lucy's tone seemed to distress the pup further, and he began to howl mournfully.

A webbed hand reached up from the dark hole and gently touched Fido's left front paw. Despite the approaching chaos, Lucy felt a sense of peace descend. Fido stopped howling and licked the brown-green finger on his paw.

"I will take the dog," said Ædifex, his voice resonating in the underground chamber.

"Got it," said Scott briefly as he carefully lowered Fido down to Ædifex. Then Scott lightly jumped down into the hole.

"Ready, Lucy?" he called up.

"Yeah, okay," she replied grimly.

Lucy sat on the edge of the hole and slung her legs over the side. Scott was standing below her, arms outstretched to catch her. Lucy sighed and pushed off, jumping down and into Scott's arms.

"Thank you," she breathed in his ear as he held her close.

"No problem," he whispered back. He gently lowered her down.

Lucy gasped as her feet sank into the cold muck.

If they can do it, so can you, she told herself firmly.

Fido gave Lucy a small yip of welcome, and she looked curiously at Ædifex.

"Did you do something with your mind to calm him down?"

"Of course. Telepathy is highly effective on animals. Not really to 'talk,' per se, but to affect their mood and make them more willing to do your bidding. Haven't you found you have a gift for handling animals?"

Lucy thought for a moment. "I guess I did feel like my pet rat, Bentley, always understood me and what I wanted. And I was pretty surprised that Fido, here, was so easy to take from the wild."

"From the wild? You mean he is a wild dog?" asked Ædifex in surprise.

"A wolf pup, actually," Lucy confessed.

"You are very gifted, then," said Ædifex. "Like me."

Modest, too, thought Lucy, suppressing a grin.

"That would explain how Romi and Remi became part of the wolf pack so quickly," Scott said thoughtfully. "They probably recognized their powers over animals a long time ago."

I don't know why I couldn't figure it out on my own! Lucy thought in annoyance.

They did have two brains between them, interjected Ædifex telepathically.

196

A Doorway Through Time

Scott interrupted their thoughts. "What should we do now, Ædifex? Can you probe the minds of the crowd above? How long do you think we'll have to wait here?"

"I could probe their minds, but I doubt I'd find any coherent thoughts," returned Ædifex. "And I have no intention of waiting here until things settle down. I'm going to use these tunnels to get us safely away from here. But first, we must hide our escape route from others. Lucy, you must take Fido now."

He handed the leashed pup to Lucy, who promptly set him down in the tunnel. Fido began sniffing the floor of the tunnel with evident interest.

"This place doesn't seem to bother him," Lucy remarked.

"He's a member of the dog family," Scott replied. "And you know how much dogs like sniffing other dogs. Yuck..."

"I know what you mean," Lucy interrupted. "Fido, you're gross!"

Fido looked up in surprise and gave a small bark, as if in agreement.

Meanwhile, Ædifex had pulled two small stones out of the leather bag that hung from his belt.

"Scott, get the torch hanging on the wall behind you," he ordered.

Scott grabbed a metal torch from the wall. The top of the torch was formed into a basin, which held a pool of oil.

Ædifex held the stones up to the torch and began striking one against the other.

Flint, Lucy realized as sparks began to fly.

Several of the sparks landed in the oil at the top of the torch, which blazed into life.

"There," said Ædifex with satisfaction. "Now we can put the sewer cover back on. Scott?"

Scott stood on tiptoes and reached for the cover. Once the lid was back in place, the sewer seemed even more oppressive, its odor weighing heavily in the stifling atmosphere. Lucy gave a little shiver.

I hope Ædifex knows what he's doing, she thought.

Of course I know what I'm doing, he answered telepathically. *I built this sewer system, and I know it like the back of my hand.*

"It is time to go. Are you ready?" Ædifex said aloud.

"Very!" replied Scott. Lucy remained silent, somewhat abashed at having revealed her thoughts.

"All right then. Follow me!"

Lucy knew she would have nightmares about these tunnels. The dark, narrow space triggered her claustrophobia, and it took all her willpower to keep her anxiety in check. The stench was nearly unbearable. Once, Lucy accidentally took a breath through her nose, and the fumes made her retch. She fought the impulse to vomit and just barely succeeded. The wet muck squelched unpleasantly underfoot, and they all had to dodge the occasional outflow from pipes draining into the tunnel. Adding to their misery were the squeaks and scratches of the resident rats, invisible in the shadows.

They're Bentley's cousins, that's all, Lucy told herself firmly.

She was startled by a yell from Scott and furious barking from Fido.

"What's wrong?" she cried.

"Rat—big as Fido—ran over my foot," Scott answered shortly.

He hates this as much as I do, thought Lucy in astonishment.

The thought gave her strength, and she followed Ædifex with new energy as he unhesitatingly jogged through the twisting maze of interconnected tunnels. He turned off into a dry corridor and slowed to a walk.

"Are we there yet?" Lucy asked hopefully.

"We are even now at the door. Stop for a moment," Ædifex replied.

Lucy could hear Ædifex rummaging in his leather pocket again.

"Aha! Here is the key," he said finally.

"Why a key?" asked Scott. "What are you protecting in the sewer?"

"You will see," said Ædifex mysteriously.

Lucy heard the click of the key turning in a lock, followed by the squeak of a wooden door opening on rusty hinges. Ædifex went through first and turned to hold the door open for the others. With the torch facing her instead of lighting the way ahead, Lucy got a good look at the others, bedraggled and stinking in the flickering light.

"We look nasty," she declared.

Scott let out a whoop of laughter. "Why don't you say what you really think, Lucy?"

"Didn't she just do that?" asked Ædifex in confusion.

"It's irony," Lucy explained. "Never mind."

"Very well. Excuse me while I lock the door behind us."

Lucy and Scott flattened themselves against the wall while Ædifex squeezed past and locked the door from the inside. He picked up the torch in his left hand, and pointed forward with his right.

"Go ahead a bit, and you will see."

Scott looked at Lucy and shrugged.

"Okay, I'll go first," Lucy said. She marched determinedly down the brick tunnel.

To her surprise, after a few yards she felt a cold draft. She felt her own tense body suddenly relax as she stepped into a vast, open space.

I didn't realize how hard I was fighting the claustrophobia, she thought.

Scott and Ædifex drew up close behind her, and the torch threw the enormous room into stark relief. Stretching before them were dozens of elegant metallic capsules, gleaming in the flickering light.

A Doorway Through Time

"Whoa," said Scott. "Are these—?"

"Spaceships," finished Ædifex proudly. "All capable of warping space or time. This room was once filled with hundreds of ships. Most Akwatairs have gone home, as I told you. There is one ship remaining for each Akwatair who is still on Earth, ensuring that we always have a way to return to Tairran."

Lucy looked hopefully at Ædifex. "Did you say these ships can travel through time?"

Ædifex smiled broadly. "I did."

"Does this mean you'll take us into the future to help us save my dad?" Lucy ventured.

"My destiny lies here, Lucy OppelLo," Ædifex said seriously. He gathered her hands in his, and Lucy felt the familiar, cool dampness of Akwatairran hands. "I love my fiancée, the beautiful Agrippina. I love my life here on Earth. I will never return to Tairran."

Then why is he torturing us like this? wondered Lucy sorrowfully.

"I am not trying to torture you, Lucy," Ædifex said quietly. "I am trying to give you my ship."

Lucy pulled her hands away and threw her arms around Ædifex. Scott stifled a laugh at the sight of Ædifex's astonished expression.

"Oh, thank you, Ædifex!" Lucy exclaimed. "I just know this time I'll save my father!"

"Yes, we will. After all, third time's the charm," murmured Scott, putting an arm around her waist.

Lucy swiveled and gave Scott a quick, fierce hug. When she stepped back, her face was shining with tears of happiness. She quickly wiped her eyes with the back of her arm and turned back to Ædifex.

"Can you show us how to fly it?"

"Of course! Come with me."

Ædifex led Lucy and Scott to a ship at the back of the room.

"There's no door. How do you get in?" Lucy asked.

"There is a door. You just have to know how to find it," Ædifex replied. "Watch me."

He stood close to the ship and placed both hands on the side. The metal skin seemed to shiver, and before their eyes, a mark appeared just above Ædifex's head. The mark soon morphed into a line that traveled clockwise until a large oval seam had formed. Then, the seam became a pocket door that slipped silently open.

"The door responds to the heat of your hands," Ædifex explained as they stepped through the entrance.

"Nice," Scott commented. He looked over at the windshield. A single chair was positioned in front of a semi-circular wheel and a bank of imposing controls. "Hey—there's only one seat!"

"These ships were intended to be one man—or woman—vessels. There should be at least one spare seat somewhere, though." Ædifex ran an exploratory hand along the floor of the ship near the captain's chair. He shook his head and frowned, then tried the ship's wall. "Ah, here it is!"

Ædifex stuck a finger through a small loop, and a narrow, hard seat pulled out from the side.

Lucy turned to Scott. "Can I drive?" she asked sweetly.

Scott hesitated and looked longingly at the controls.

He really wants to fly it, Lucy realized. *But I want to be in charge of rescuing my dad.*

Scott is a pilot by profession, Ædifex interrupted her telepathically. *It's only natural he would want to fly it, too.*

Lucy closed her mind and glared at Ædifex.

Time to be a big girl, she decided.

"Maybe we could split the driving?" she offered in a strained voice.

Scott's face lit up in delight. "That would be perfect!" He took Lucy in his arms for a long, grateful kiss.

It was worth making him so happy! Lucy told herself.

"Okay, but me first!" Lucy said when they came up for air.

Ædifex was standing with his arms crossed, foot tapping in impatience.

"Are you finally ready for your lesson?" Ædifex asked.

"Yeah, sorry, Ædifex," Scott apologized.

"Since you're going first, have a seat at the wheel,

Lucy, and both of you watch carefully."

Lucy got settled in the chair, and Scott drew near. Ædifex pointed at a square on the control panel that glimmered with small, sparkling dots.

"This is your map. You can program the ship to go anywhere in the known universe. Since you want to stay on Earth, that makes it easy."

He pressed a finger on the square, and the windshield was overlaid with a huge star map of the Milky Way galaxy.

"There's the Big Dipper!" Lucy exclaimed. "Uh, Ursa Major," she added, remembering her Latin.

"And Orion, and Ursa Minor," Scott added.

"Which are all well and good," Ædifex interjected, "but you want to remain in your own solar system, here." He put his thumb and first finger together, and touched them to an insignificant-looking star. As he spread them apart, the map zoomed in, showing eight planets orbiting a star. "Your sun and its planets."

"Named for Roman gods," Lucy murmured.

"Is that so?" Ædifex said with delight. "How wonderful!"

"I suppose so," Lucy agreed. "Okay, I think I can guess what comes next."

She leaned forward and tapped the third planet with her finger. The map zoomed in so that now a perfect image of the Earth rotated before their eyes. Ædifex reached in front of her and touched the European continent when it appeared, stopping the Earth's rotation. He was about to zoom in on the boot of Italy when Scott put a hand on his arm to stop him.

"We don't actually live in Italy," Scott explained. "Lucy's dad will be taking off on a different continent."

Ædifex stood up straight in astonishment. "Indeed! I can't imagine why you would want to live somewhere else. Very well. Simply put a finger on the Earth and drag to rotate the image until you see your continent."

Scott leaned in and turned the image until North America came into view. He was about to touch the Florida peninsula when he paused in confusion.

"It hasn't been settled yet, so I can't pick the space center," he said disconcertedly.

"Don't worry, Scott, we can just take a best guess and figure it out when we get there," Lucy said breezily. "Anyway, I think it's about here." She reached up and touched a spot in the center of the peninsula on the east coast. A spot of light glowed where she had touched it.

"Tap it again to lock in your location," Ædifex advised.

Lucy touched the spot again, and a string of symbols appeared on the dashboard above the map button.

"Latitude and longitude in Akwatairran numbers?" Scott guessed.

Ædifex inclined his head. "Exactly. We have set the place, so now we must set the time. That is where it gets tricky. The ship can automatically calculate the length of an Earth day based on the size of your planet and its distance from the sun. However, you need to tell it how many days in the future to go. The ship has a calculator I can help you use."

"Go for it, Scott! I know that today is March 15, 44 BC, and that we need to get to March 31, 2064 AD, but that's about all I know," Lucy said. "I'll let you sit in the fancy chair while you two figure it out."

She left Scott and Ædifex earnestly discussing the modern calendar and the necessity of accounting for leap years.

"C'mon, Fido," Lucy said, breaking into English. "Let's see what's at the back of this ship." She gave a small tug on Fido's leash, and he willingly followed as she found the door to a storeroom.

"Check it out!" Lucy cried in delight. "Extra clothes! And cupboards with... food?" She opened a box and sniffed suspiciously. "Smells awfully fishy," she grumbled. "Akwatairs have strange tastes."

She ran her hand along the back of the storeroom, and another door formed. Lucy poked her head in, and a light came on. "A bathroom with running water! Excellent!"

Lucy quickly removed her soiled toga and sandals and did her best to wash her filthy feet. She pulled on a spare robe that covered her from shoulders to toes.

"Mmm, I'd forgotten how wonderful Akwatairran clothes feel," she told Fido. The light teal cloth rippled and flowed delightfully on her skin. Fido seemed to agree with Lucy and stepped closer to her.

"Watch out, buddy!" she warned. "You need to get cleaned up, too."

Lucy gingerly lifted Fido and placed him in the basin. He laid his ears back and growled, but submitted to her ministrations. Lucy focused on his legs and feet, scrubbing for several minutes until she felt satisfied and set him back on the floor.

"Much better," she declared. "Now we're presentable."

"Lucy!" called Scott. "What are you up to?"

"C'mon back," she replied. "You can wash up and get new clothes."

Lucy returned to the front while Scott took his turn. Before long, he returned in a clean, purple Akwatairran robe.

"You should wear purple dresses more often," Lucy told Scott. "It suits your complexion."

"Shut up," he growled good-naturedly.

"So how does this ship work?" asked Lucy, turning to Ædifex. "Can we take off from here?"

"Not exactly," Ædifex explained with a smile. "You first have to launch the ship into outer space—or at least the upper atmosphere." He put his hands on the ship's wheel to demonstrate. "Start the engine by pulling out the wheel; stop the engine by pushing the wheel back into the dashboard. You pull the wheel in the direction you want to move: up,

207

down, left, or right. The pedals by your feet let you increase your speed, slow down, or put the ship in a holding position." He pointed to each pedal as he named it.

"Great," groaned Lucy. "It's the opposite in a hover-car. I hope I don't mess up!"

"Believe in yourself," Ædifex said calmly. "I do."

Lucy blushed. "Thanks."

"If you drive the ship to the back of the room," Ædifex continued, "you will find yourself in a long tunnel that opens into a remote part of the country. From there, fly up as high as you comfortably can. Stop the ship and press the red button, here, just below the map symbol on your dashboard. You will hear some strange sounds and feel some heat as the ship projects a massive amount of energy to create a rotating black hole. Enter the hole, and in a few moments, you will be in the land of Flo-ree-da," he pronounced awkwardly.

"Wait a minute, a black hole? Won't we be crushed by it?" asked Lucy in horror.

"A typical black hole is a singularity in space where gravity is so intense that not even light can escape; if you entered it, you would indeed be captured and crushed. But I am talking about a rotating black hole. I don't know exactly how it is done." He waved a webbed hand blithely in the air. "That is a matter for the physicists of Tairran. What I do know is that it is completely safe to enter this kind. The creation of the rotating black hole automatically produces its inverse twin: a white hole. You exit through the white hole to the time and place you specified."

"Incredible," Lucy said solemnly.

"Dr. Hartwick is going to love taking a look at this baby," Scott whispered.

Ædifex drew himself up to his full height. "Do you understand what you need to do? I know this has been a lot of information."

Lucy and Scott looked at one another and nodded.

"I think between the two of us we'll be fine," Lucy answered.

"Very well then. I would have liked more time to know you both better. I wish you could have met my future wife. But I understand you are on a mission. May all the gods be with you."

"Thank you so much for everything, Ædifex," Lucy replied. She stood and hugged him one last time.

"Thank you," added Scott. Scott stuck out his right hand, and after a moment of confused hesitation, Ædifex shook it warmly.

With a bow and a wave, Ædifex stepped out of the ship. The door closed silently behind him as Lucy and Scott buckled themselves in.

"Wait, where should we put Fido?" Lucy asked.

"I'll double-buckle with him," Scott decided.

Fido was nosing about the floor of the cabin, searching for crumbs. Scott scooped him up and soon had the pup settled in his lap with the seatbelt stretched over both of them. Scott turned to Lucy.

"The time and place coordinates are set. How about you—are you ready?"

"Absolutely!" she returned. "Like you said, third time's the charm."

Chapter 17

✲ ✲ ✲

Lucy pulled the wheel from the dashboard, and the ship's engine rumbled to life. She gently pulled up on the wheel, and the ship rose a few inches off the ground.

"So far, so good," she said aloud.

She turned the wheel toward the back of the room and pressed her foot on the middle pedal. The ship shot forward, and Lucy tried to slow it by jamming on the right pedal. The ship stopped so suddenly that Lucy and Scott were jolted forward in their seats, then painfully snapped back into place by their seatbelts. Fido yelped in pain.

"Sorry, Fido," Lucy apologized. "And Scott."

"Could've happened to anyone," Scott said quickly. "Try again."

Lucy tried to push the forward pedal gently, but her foot slipped, and she ended up pushing it down hard. She panicked and stepped quickly on the brake. The ship bucked in place up and down, and the seatbelts cut into their shoulders again. Fido whimpered, and Lucy looked

211

hesitantly at Scott. His mouth was set in a grim line, but he didn't say anything.

I can't fail, Lucy told herself.

She wiped her sweaty hands on her robe and gripped the wheel once again. She pressed the pedal down very gently, and this time the ship moved forward smoothly. The ship's sensors automatically turned on powerful head-lights, so Lucy could easily see the tunnel to the outside. It was very long, low, and narrow.

There's no way I can get through that without scrap-ing the sides of the ship, she decided. *Time to salvage this situation.*

She carefully tapped the leftmost pedal, and the ship hovered in place.

"I changed my mind," she told Scott airily. "This is the boring part. I'd rather drive on the way home."

Scott grinned. "Of course, if that's what you'd prefer."

"Yes, I believe I would," she answered with all the pride she could muster.

Slowly and deliberately, Lucy rose from her seat and switched places with Scott.

"You're sitting with me," she told Fido firmly.

His ears flattened in disagreement, but Lucy won the day and finally secured the seatbelt around herself and the complaining pup.

"Okay, let's see what she can do," Scott said with en-thusiasm as he eased the ship down the tunnel.

"I don't see why people call ships 'she.' It's ridiculous," Lucy complained.

Scott gave her a sideways look. "Fine. I know. We'll call it 'he.'"

"It."

"You're a little ridiculous."

"No, you're a little ridiculous."

Before Scott could reply, a shaft of light appeared ahead, widening as the tunnel's exit opened in response to the ship's approach.

"Pretty slick," Scott said admiringly.

In a moment, they flew out of the tunnel and over a desolate, rocky plain. Scott pulled back hard on the wheel and pressed the pedal down to the floor. The ship shot up at a nearly 90° angle. Lucy was sitting on the right side wall of the ship, so while Scott was merely pressed back into his seat, Lucy had to clutch the right arm of her chair to stay balanced and keep the seatbelt from cutting into her skin.

It's just for a few minutes, she told herself, gritting her teeth. Her arm muscles were straining and burning.

Scott looked over and noticed her distress. He quickly tilted the wheel to reduce the severity of their upward climb. Lucy exhaled in relief as she relaxed her arms.

"Sorry, Luce," Scott said contritely. "I was enjoying the power of this thing."

"It's okay," she replied. "Just get us into position."

213

The ship continued to climb, and in a few moments, it burst through a layer of clouds. Scott pushed down on the wheel to level out the ship and pressed the left pedal to put it in a holding position.

"I forgot to ask Ædifex if we'd spin when we enter the black hole. Do you remember what you need to do if the ship starts spinning?" he asked

"After the wormhole adventures, I'll never forget," Lucy answered. "Pick a point straight ahead of me and focus on it."

"Good. Here we go."

Scott pressed the red button on the dashboard. A humming noise emanated from the base of the ship. It got louder with each passing second, and Lucy felt her seat and the air around her begin to get warmer. Soon she felt sweat begin to bead up on her forehead. Fido was whining, trying to escape the grip of the belt.

"Ædifex did say this would happen, right?" she asked nervously.

"He did, but man, this is miserable."

Their discomfort was forgotten as three beams of light suddenly appeared before them, flowing outward from the ship and converging in a single point. The point of light intensified as the seconds passed, as though a tiny star were forming before their very eyes. Lucy squinted and shielded her eyes. Just when she thought she could no longer bear the brightness, the star imploded. Waves of

214

light and heat rippled out, rocking the ship and pushing it back. The light went out, but when Lucy closed her eyes, the light had left its imprint on her eyelids, and she could see the star as clearly as though it were still there. The ship hung suspended in space for a long moment, then slowly began moving forward.

"Are you making it do that?" Lucy whispered.

"No, it's moving on its own," Scott replied, his voice full of tension. "Get ready."

The ship picked up speed and was soon hurtling forward. Seconds later, they were engulfed in absolute blackness.

"What happened to the headlights?" Lucy asked in panic.

"They're still on. The black hole must suck up the light as soon as it forms."

The ship began to groan as the metallic sides bowed inward. Lucy felt intense pressure all over her body. She could feel her skin and bones pushing against her innards, crushing her organs.

"I—I can't breathe!" she gasped.

"Small breaths. Not... too fast," Scott choked out.

Lucy gripped the arms of her chair. Fido was silent and motionless.

Can Ædifex really be right? Can humans survive this? Maybe it only works if you're an Akwatair, Lucy wondered frantically. *And what about Fido?*

215

Judith Bourassa Joy

The pressure and pain became insufferable. Lucy opened her mouth to scream, but she could not draw enough breath. Her vision darkened as her body shut down.

I'm going to faint, she realized.

And then it stopped. Light suffused the ship, and Lucy watched in amazement as her hands regained their normal plumpness. She tried to draw a breath and gasped over and over, unable to fill her lungs.

I got the wind knocked out of me, just like Marius, she realized. *I will breathe again, I will breathe again,* she told herself, fighting the waves of panic.

At last, she actually could draw a deep breath. Lucy relaxed and opened her eyes wide in astonishment. The ship was spinning, now bathed in a sea of light.

Focus on a single point, Lucy told herself as she stared firmly at a small stain on the floor of the ship.

The light vanished as quickly as it appeared, and Lucy saw that the ship was rolling in a blue sky, wispy clouds drifting ahead. Scott was pulling on the wheel, fighting to right the ship and keep it level. With one last, mighty effort, he succeeded.

"We survived," he said triumphantly, wiping the sweat from his brow.

Lucy was about to reply, when, instead, she paused in surprise. "We might not," she answered numbly, pointing ahead.

A Doorway Through Time

A jet was bearing down on them. Scott swore and pushed down hard on both the wheel and the forward pedal. The spaceship tipped down and sped toward Earth, rocking as it fell in the wake of the jet.

"We'd better hope we don't hit any little pleasure planes," Scott said.

"Jinx," answered Lucy.

Scott swore again and began jerking the wheel, swiveling and turning to avoid the small planes in their path.

"Everyone must be out sightseeing on this beautiful day," Lucy remarked between gritted teeth.

"Let's hope we're going so fast they think they imagined us," Scott answered without taking his eyes off the windshield. "I'm going to glide a couple hundred feet off the ocean, so we're off the radar, but we don't clip any ships. North? South? Where do you think we are? You're the one who wanted to 'figure it out when we got here.'"

"South. The way you're headed," Lucy said, ignoring his tone.

Her confidence fell as the minutes passed. The sight of a distant chain of large islands to her left confirmed Lucy's fears.

"I think we should have seen the space center by now," she admitted. "I'm, uh, pretty sure those are the Bahamas over on our left."

Scott squinted into the distance to see where Lucy was pointing. He groaned and turned the ship around.

"I didn't see Mr. Boy Scout acting like a navigation genius. At least I noticed before we got to Cuba," Lucy muttered under her breath.

Scott's mouth twitched, but he remained silent. After about fifteen minutes, a huge tower could be seen in the distance on the edge of the coast.

"That's it! That's the space center, and there's Dad's ship, ready to launch. Hurry up!"

"What do you think I've been doing?" Scott grumbled.

He turned the ship toward land and angled into a hovercar lane. Lucy laughed out loud to see the astonished faces of other travelers.

"They're impressed by our new wings!" she cried.

Scott grinned, cheerful again. "We've got the best vehicle on Earth right now. Let's hope we don't get pulled over—Ædifex didn't give us a registration," he joked.

They soon reached the space center and dropped out of the air highway and into the lot, deciding they would try to let the ship blend in with the army of buses at the edge. They emerged, blinking in the bright, humid air, and set off at a run. Fido jogged along beside them.

"He looks glad to be outside again," Scott observed.

"Me, too," Lucy replied absentmindedly, more interested in the events at hand. "There's a huge crowd gathered at the base of the ship. It must be nearly ready for launch, so the crew is probably saying their good-byes to their families inside the center. In fact, I must be inside the center!" she concluded in surprise.

"That's right, you're in two places at once. Better make sure the other Lucy doesn't see you. Maybe your dad shouldn't see you, either."

"But I haven't talked to my dad in years!" Lucy cried.

"I know," Scott said sympathetically, "but we won't have much time to convince him about the bomb. We need to focus on saving his life, not explaining time travel."

Lucy paused, wanting to argue, then sighed. "All right," she said begrudgingly. "Let's join the crowd. You need to get Dad's attention when he walks past to board."

They ran quickly now, without talking, until they reached the mass of people waiting to cheer on the astronauts.

How are we ever going to get to the front? Lucy wondered. *I've never been part of the crowd before.*

In her hurry, she began pushing and elbowing her way forward, ignoring the complaints and curses of those around her. Fido followed in her path, with Scott close behind. Lucy reached the front of the crowd just in time to see Henry Starrett's bright red hair, nearly the same color as his jumpsuit, as he followed the crew toward the ship. Lucy was just about to call out when her head was assaulted with a white-hot sensation. She took a step back, reeling in pain.

It can't be, she thought in astonishment.

219

Judith Bourassa Joy

A figure, ostensibly a maintenance worker, emerged from the base of the ship. His head was covered with a hood, but he turned to stare at Lucy with round, amber eyes. Lucy shivered, sensing his turbulent emotions.

Why would an Akwatair be here? Why now? she wondered. Lucy couldn't help herself and quickly probed his mind. The answer became clear.

"Mr. Starrett!" Scott shouted next to her.

"Dad! Dad!" Lucy shrieked, suddenly remembering her mission.

Henry Starrett had reached the base of the stairs and had one foot on the first step. Lucy's and Scott's voices were washed away by the cheers of the people all around, and Henry showed no sign of stopping.

I just can't be too late! Not after all I've been through, she thought in desperation.

Fido sensed Lucy's unhappiness and began to howl. His shrill voice pierced through the roar of the crowd, and Henry hesitated at the peculiar sound. He turned his head and looked back.

Scott was jumping up and down and waving his arms.

"Dad!" Lucy screamed again. Henry squinted and looked toward her. She hid quickly behind Scott, crouching down and letting the throng of people conceal her. Scott beckoned, and Henry walked toward them. Lucy forced herself to stay out of sight.

Dad is alive! Lucy was ecstatic. Tears of joy began to

stream down her face.

Henry drew close and people nearby began screaming in delight, trying to touch him for luck. Security guards quickly appeared, surrounding Henry, but he motioned them aside.

"Mr. Starrett, I—" Scott began, but Henry wasn't listening.

"I thought I heard my daughter," Henry muttered, scanning the crowd with a puzzled expression.

"Mr. Starrett, I'm here to help you. I'm a friend of Lucy's," Scott said earnestly. Henry turned to face him at the sound of Lucy's name. "I'm an officer with the Space Brigadiers. We just received a tip that there's a bomb aboard the *Icarus*."

"But the ship has already been checked," Henry replied, rubbing his forehead anxiously.

Scott leaned in closer. "Sir, I know it sounds crazy, but we're certain it's true. If you want to survive this trip and get back to your family, you need to believe me."

Henry looked doubtful, but he nodded. "Okay," he agreed, "I'll have them check again." He gave Scott a long look and then stepped back to pull aside one of the guards.

Lucy stood upright and leaned against Scott in relief.

"We did it. They're going to make another security sweep," Scott told her in a strained voice.

"What's wrong?" Lucy asked in concern. *He looks really pale,* she realized.

"I feel kind of funny," he admitted.

"Let's get you back to the ship right away, so you can rest," she said quickly. "Dad is going to be okay now."

"That's great! You did it," he answered with a weak smile.

"We did it. Now let's go."

It was a laborious journey back to the ship. Scott moved more and more slowly and had to pause every few minutes. Lucy had her arm around him for support and felt his weight leaning more heavily on her with every step.

"This sure... came on... suddenly," Scott gasped out.

I don't think I can hold him if he faints, Lucy thought, eyeing his tall frame.

She was momentarily distracted by the sight of a contingent of soldiers descending on the station.

"That must be the bomb squad," she realized. "Thank goodness."

Scott murmured something unintelligible, and Lucy strengthened her hold on him. They finally made it to the ship, and Lucy helped Scott into his side seat.

"It's a good thing you decided to drive on the way home," Scott said quietly as she buckled him and Fido into the chair.

He's so pale, he looks almost transparent, Lucy realized in alarm.

"Yup, and when we get home, I'll take you to a modern doctor. No more antique healers, like Crispus," Lucy said in an attempt at humor.

Scott closed his eyes.

Right, it's up to me to get us out of here and help Scott.

The thought gave Lucy strength and determination, and Ædifex's driving lesson came back to her clearly. Lucy started the ship and glided out of the lot, but this time, avoided the hovercar lanes. Instead, she headed straight toward the water and up. Once she had passed the beach, she glanced at the sky.

No planes nearby, she reassured herself.

She pulled back hard on the wheel and headed up for several minutes before putting the ship in a holding position. *Higher than the small planes, lower than the big ones,* she decided. *Perfect.*

She touched the map button on the dashboard, and the globe of Earth appeared with their last setting, the Florida peninsula, in view. Lucy reached forward and quickly turned Earth until Italy appeared. A number of dots glowed all over the continents of Europe, Africa and Asia.

Because the Akwatairs had mapped those cities back in 44 BC, she realized. *And there is Rome! I can get back to the villa easily from there.*

She glanced over at Scott, who was slumped in his seat, held upright only by the strength of his seatbelt. *And I'd better get there fast. Good thing Scott and Ædifex already programmed in the correct date.*

Lucy repeated the steps Scott had followed, and once

again, the ship grew uncomfortably warm as the energy beams fired up. Lucy glanced from the star that was quickly forming back to Scott. His eyes were closed, and his face was pale and glistening with sweat. Fido lay miserably across Scott's lap, breathing in gasping pants.

"My poor boys," said Lucy softly, forgetting her own discomfort.

She turned her gaze back to the new star, fascinated again to see one forming before her. She closed her eyes when it became unbearably bright.

Time for the big explosion, she thought. *At least I know what's coming this time.*

Again, the ship was buffeted back by the energy waves, then drawn faster and faster into the invisible blackness.

I hope Scott survives the squeezing, Lucy thought anxiously as her eyeballs seemed to press against her brain.

At last, they emerged into and out of the light. The ship was hovering above the city of Rome.

"There's the Vatican!" Lucy exclaimed. "Scott, we're home!"

A mournful howl erupted from the side of the ship. Lucy looked over in alarm. Fido was cowering below an empty seat. Scott had disappeared.

Chapter 18
꙳ ꙳ ꙳

"But I've already explained the whole thing!" Lucy shouted. She was seated in a large leather armchair with her knees tucked under her chin and her arms wrapped around her long legs.

"I know, dear, but you were mumbling again and not really making sense," Ellen said soothingly. She glanced nervously at her husband and leaned over to feel Lucy's forehead. "You're so warm, but look at you! You're shaking like a leaf!"

"She was lost outside for hours," Dr. Hartwick commented soberly across the large living room. "It's probably heatstroke. She may be shaking with fever chills."

"I wasn't lost," Lucy said adamantly. "Just ask Romi or Remi," she added sarcastically. "You'll have to go back in time a few thousand years, but maybe then you'll believe me."

Henry, Ellen, and Dr. Hartwick exchanged nervous looks.

"Lucy," Ellen began slowly, "Romi and Remi are in

Indonesia. Don't you remember? They behaved so badly
that we had to send them back to their parents. Your Aunt
Rhea just picked them up at the airport."

"But that can't be right!" Lucy exclaimed.

Henry cautiously approached his daughter with a tall
glass of ice water. "There, there, Lucy," he said quietly.
"Try to sip a little of this."

I can't take it anymore! Lucy thought furiously. *I'm not
crazy, and I'm not sick. Why can't anyone understand me?*

Lucy uncoiled herself from the chair and sprang up.
"I'm fine, but I'm hot because I just got off a spaceship
where I was sitting while a star formed and collapsed! I'll
show you my ship and prove it to you!" She turned to Dr.
Hartwick beseechingly. "It works the way you wished you
could make your time machine work. It creates a rotating
black hole first and a white hole afterward. That way you
can safely travel through time and space."

"That's fascinating, Lucy! But what do you mean, my
time machine? I've never built any such thing."

"What are you talking about?" Lucy gasped. "That's
why you're here at this secret laboratory!"

The three adults exchanged worried glances.

"Noooo," Henry said slowly and carefully. "We're
here working on cloaking devices for military aircraft."

Lucy reached down to pat Fido, who lay quietly at
her feet. "You're real, Fido. And I do have an alien spaceship hidden up on the hill that's real, too, if you would

all just believe me and come see. I feel like Dorothy when she came back from Oz. It all happened the way I said, I swear it!"

Lucy looked at the faces of the three adults ranged before her. She saw concern, love, and... doubt.

"Aargh!" she cried out in frustration. "Fine! I'll find someone who understands me."

Lucy turned on her heel and ran for her room, Fido in close pursuit. She could hear her father's voice, faint behind her.

"Don't go after her, Ellen. I think she needs some time alone."

He's right about that anyway, Lucy thought in chagrin. She rounded the corner and opened the nearest door.

"My bedroom—at least something's still the same!" she exclaimed aloud in relief.

Lucy headed for her bureau and began flinging clothing out of the top drawer. Fido yelped as a pair of socks hit him in the face.

"Sorry, Fido," Lucy apologized. "I've got to find Sayesha's number. Aha! Got it!"

Lucy fished the battered business card from the bottom corner of the drawer.

"U101-1313-1313," she said under her breath. "How could I forget, lucky 13?"

Minutes later, Lucy was looking at Sayesha's concerned face on the videophone.

227

Judith Bourassa Joy

"Sayesha, I just had the most incredible adventure, and now I've come back and no one believes it happened! And Scott has disappeared and I—"

"Wait, wait!" Sayesha begged. "I cannot understand so much English so fast. Think what you have to say, Lucy."

So Lucy telepathically described the events of the past few days while Sayesha listened intently.

I don't understand why some things are the same, and some are different, Lucy concluded. *Why is Fido here, but Scott is not? Is Scott lost somewhere? Why do you believe me, but my parents don't?*

Sayesha replied with gentle good humor, *Maybe I believe you because it is too fantastic a story for me to hear from a stranger and not believe.*

Lucy paused for a moment, trying to take in Sayesha's thoughts. *What do you mean, 'from a stranger?'* Lucy demanded.

We have never met, Lucy Starrett, Sayesha replied. *I have never seen you before.*

"Then how did I have your business card?"

Sayesha shrugged. *Maybe in this alternate reality, you picked it up on the floor of a train station and kept it out of curiosity. Maybe the card was here, waiting for you. I do not know. All I know is that things like this do not happen by chance. We were destined to know each other.*

Lucy hesitated. *Then you believe everything I've told you?*

228

A Doorway Through Time

Of course I do. I can look into your mind, as you know, and see that it is honest, brave, and pure. Sayesha gazed into Lucy's eyes and smiled. *I have experienced many strange things in my life, Lucy,* she continued. *Admittedly, this is one of the strangest. But it cannot be a coincidence that when you call me now, I am not far from you. I am in Italy, too. I am a guest speaker at a telepath convention in Milan.*

Could you visit me? Lucy pleaded. *Help my family understand?*

I will leave on the first train out. Give me your address. And Lucy, if I were you, I would begin unraveling these mysteries by checking databases for information on Scott Davenport. Perhaps he is living or working somewhere else in this reality.

Good idea! Lucy agreed. *But Sayesha, what do you mean by another reality?*

Don't you see? You have altered the forces of space and time. You have created a tear in one universe and emerged into a parallel universe where things are much the same... but also very different.

Lucy shivered with an uneasy premonition. *Thank you so much Sayesha. For everything. I'll see you tomorrow.*

Lucy ended the videophone connection and quickly shifted the screen mode to a computer display.

"Scott Edward Davenport, born November 27, 2046. All records," Lucy said aloud.

Lines of text swiftly appeared and Lucy scrolled to find the most recent hit.

April 1, 2064. What is it with that date? she wondered.

She touched a finger to the date to expand the news story and began reading aloud softly to herself.

"Captain Scott Davenport, pre-medical student and officer in the elite Space Brigadiers, died in a tragic hovercar accident. He was responding to an emergency alert to join his regiment in defusing a bomb on the spaceship *Icarus*."

Lucy faltered and let forth a primal scream of despair. Fido joined in, howling alongside his mistress.

"Lucy?" called a voice from the doorway. "What's wrong?"

Lucy raised a grief-stricken face and saw a welcome figure, shadowy in the doorway.

"Donald!" she cried out. "Finally, something is going right!"

Lucy burst into tears, and Donald ran into the room to embrace his sister. She leaned into her brother and sobbed for several long minutes. Then she took a long, shuddering breath and wiped her face on Donald's shoulder.

"Um, gross," he said. "Now are you going to tell me what this is all about?"

Fido whined and Donald looked over in astonishment, seeing the pup for the first time.

"Where'd he come from?" Donald asked as he extended a hand to Fido. Fido gingerly sniffed Donald's hand

and licked his fingers.

"He likes you," Lucy remarked, momentarily distracted.

"Of course he does," returned Donald. "All dogs seem to like me."

"This one's a wolf, and I got him 3,000 years ago."

"What the hell, Lucy?"

Fido's stomach growled as he lay flat on the ground, his head extended piteously.

"The poor thing is starving," Lucy said. "Let's get him something to eat and take him outside. I'll tell you everything."

After a quick stop in the kitchen, Lucy and Donald sat on a moonlit bench to talk. Lucy went on for hours while Fido inspected every inch of the kitchen garden before falling asleep at her feet. At the end of Lucy's long-winded tale, Donald shook his head in amazement.

"So let me get this straight," he said. "I stole a ship with you and went on this incredible adventure to the planet Tairran. And you became an Akwatair goddess and pretty much saved a civilization? And then you and this guy, Scott, stole a time machine and tried to warn Dad about the bomb—stopping in a couple of Romes, at different points in time, along the way?"

Fido rose, stretched, and began trotting about the garden again.

"That's right," Lucy agreed. "And despite our not-so-favorite cousins' best efforts, Scott and I did warn Dad, which is why he's alive in this universe. And why..." she faltered for a moment. "Scott is dead."

She looked over at Fido, who was lingering near a raised bed of herbs.

"Not the basil, Fido—we eat that!" Lucy called out in alarm as Fido lifted a leg.

Donald guffawed. "Better warn Renata to wash it first." He sighed and turned serious again. "Okay, now what are we going to do to fix things?"

"So you believe me?" Lucy nearly shouted in relief.

"Yeah. Even you couldn't make up a story like that. And besides, you have some amazing alien spacecraft hidden up on that hill, right? Show Mom and Dad and Dr. Hartwick, and they'll have to believe you."

"I couldn't even get them to agree to go with me," Lucy said.

"They'll go. They'll listen to me because I'm the wise older brother. Sucks to be you."

Lucy stuck out her tongue at him.

"Yeah, it does," she agreed. "Hey, Sayesha will be here in the morning! She'll back me up, too. Even if it's the first time we've met in this universe."

Donald glanced up at the sky. Pale pink streaks were lightening the gray horizon.

"It's almost morning now. I'll whip you up a home-made breakfast in our fantastic, old-fashioned kitchen."

A Doorway Through Time

"I told Scott you'd love that," Lucy said happily as she took her brother's arm and headed back inside with him, Fido at her heels.

Chapter 19

Lucy was chewing on a thick piece of homemade toast with fresh butter when Ellen and Henry Starrett quietly entered the kitchen.

"How are you feeling this morning, Lucy?" Henry asked carefully.

"Fine, now that someone believes me." Lucy looked pointedly at Donald who seemed alarmed to be the center of attention.

"Yes, about that," Ellen began. "Your father and I have talked, and we know that you have always been truthful. We know that you believe your story. So we'll take a walk with you, and you can see if you can find your, um, alien spaceship."

Someone yawned hugely at the entrance to the kitchen. Lucy turned to see Dr. Hartwick, wrapped in a blue-and-white seersucker robe, rubbing his eyes and nodding in agreement.

"I'm going, too," he said. He yawned again and headed straight for the coffeemaker.

234

"We'll just grab a quick breakfast, and then will you be ready to head out? Lucy?" Ellen inquired.

Lucy's glazed expression cleared as she glanced over at her mother, suddenly aware she was being addressed.

"Sorry, Mom, I was having a telepathic conversation with my friend Sayesha. She just got in from Milan, and she's on our doorstep. Back in a sec."

Lucy bolted for the front door as Henry turned to Ellen in confusion.

"Did you hear the doorbell?" he asked his wife.

"Did you hear Lucy say she was telepathic?" Dr. Hartwick added.

"No and yes," Ellen answered. "I think it's time to bring her to some sort of doctor."

"Get with it, guys," Donald interrupted. "Didn't you know your daughter is not just a space and time traveler, but also a goddess on an alien planet... and a gifted telepath?"

"Donald, you're not funny, and you're just proving my point," Ellen began. She was interrupted by the appearance of Lucy and a large woman of African descent, who was dressed in a brightly colored robe and hat.

"Donald, Dad, Mom, Dr. Hartwick, this is Sayesha Herero. We're good friends in an alternate universe. She's the head of the Northeast Order of Telepaths in that other reality—in this one, too?"

Sayesha nodded and laughed. "Yes, that much is being the same."

Ellen interjected hesitantly, "Do you... know what Lucy's talking about, Ms. Herero? I.... apologize for this talk of alternate universes."

Sayesha turned serious. "You are not believing? I have just met your daughter in this universe, Mrs. Starrett, but I believe I would be knowing her in any universe. Our—" Sayesha hesitated to find the right word— "souls are destined to meet and help one another. We can read each other's minds, and I am being excited by her stories. I believe I have a role to play in her next adventure."

Ellen and Henry exchanged looks.

Uh-oh, Lucy realized with a sinking feeling. *They think she's totally crazy.*

"Well, thank you for coming, Sayesha, and for believing in me," Lucy said pointedly. "Have you had breakfast? You can join us."

Sayesha beamed. "Thank you, I am having much hunger in my belly."

Lucy rushed to get Sayesha some breakfast while Ellen, Henry, and Dr. Hartwick found something to eat as well. As they ate, Lucy summarized her trip to Akwatair and related the story of her time travel in vivid detail.

"Whatever happens, you have the makings of a great novelist, Lucy," Henry commented at the end.

"I know it sounds incredible, but—wait! I've got pictures!" Lucy suddenly remembered. She looked around the old-fashioned kitchen in dismay. "I need to download them—but where?"

Henry reached in his pocket and pulled out a small, hand-held device.

"You can display them on this," he offered.

"Thanks," Lucy said, "but I think it would be better on a big screen. Would you all mind moving to the library?"

With murmurs of assent, they all headed for the library where Lucy swiftly downloaded her photos from the ancient Romes.

There were gasps of astonishment as the images flickered by. The rude village in ancient Rome, Marius, Romi and Remi, and the sacrificial altar all shimmered in turn on the screen.

"Our Romi and Remi—our horrible Romi and Remi—are Romulus and Remus, the founders of ancient Rome?" Ellen asked in astonishment.

"Yes, that's exactly what I'm telling you!" Lucy answered.

Sayesha nodded her head wisely. "Time and space are now being all tied up with history and destiny. You had to take your journey in time, Lucy."

The picture changed to an image of Scott next to the fountain in Caesar's Rome.

"It's Scott!" Lucy gasped. Her eyes welled with tears. "I know you're right, Sayesha, but I don't want things to be the way they are now. I don't want to give up Scott!"

"I'm thinking Romi and Remi's mama and papa would not want to give them up, either, but change we want and change we don't want always weave together." She leaned over to give Lucy's hand a sympathetic squeeze. "Maybe we can think of something."

Lucy gave her a wobbly smile.

"It's kind of funny," Donald broke in. "I know I've never met Scott, but I feel like I know him."

"You're best friends," Lucy said miserably.

"Let's just keep going," grumbled Dr. Hartwick.

Next there were pictures of Ædifex in his home, and Ellen leaned forward to get a closer look.

"There's something... very different about him," she murmured.

"His being alien?" Sayesha said.

"How did you—?" Lucy began.

Sayesha tapped the side of her head. "I just know. Am right, yes?"

"Yes," Lucy agreed admiringly. "He's from Tairran, oddly enough. It seems they settled on Earth in Roman times and showed them how to build bridges and roads and stuff."

"Not so odd," Sayesha remarked. "It is like a—how you say—tapestry. Once a connection is made, there is being many threads, many connections, weaving the two worlds together."

"All right, that's enough," Dr. Hartwick said impatiently.

A Doorway Through Time

"Enough about aliens. And when you start giving aliens credit for human genius, it really rubs me the wrong way. I don't know what's going on, but it's time to provide some concrete proof, not just pictures that could have been altered. I know you have a great sense of humor, Lucy, as well as a great imagination, and if it were April 1, I would congratulate you on the greatest April Fool's prank ever. But it's not April 1, and I have important things to do. So let's take that walk and put an end to this nonsense."

"Fine. Follow me," Lucy said stiffly as she started toward the doorway. "I like the Dr. Hartwick in the other universe better," she said in a low voice, just for Donald's benefit.

The journey took longer than expected, with Dr. Hartwick lumbering slowly along the trail. Lucy was amused to see Sayesha attempting to engage him in conversation.

They make a pretty cute couple, she thought.

They had nearly reached the summit when Lucy beckoned the group toward a dense copse of trees.

"In there," she said, pointing.

Lucy watched as the adults picked their way through the bushes and waited a beat. Her patience was soon rewarded with whoops of astonishment.

"Awesome!"

"Great Scott!"

"Good lord, it's real!"

"It's actually true!"

"I be telling you so," boomed Sayesha.

"Thanks, Sayesha. I couldn't have said it better my-self," Lucy said as she joined the group. She laid her palms on the side of the craft, and the door appeared.

"Whoa," said Donald admiringly.

"Come on in, I'll show you around," Lucy invited them.

Several hours later, the crowd had regrouped in the villa's garden for lunch under the olive trees. This time, however, everyone was engaged in animated conversation, no longer questioning Lucy's story, but searching for a res-olution to the conundrum.

"So what it boils down to is this," Ellen said. "You saved your father, but you killed your boyfriend."

Lucy winced.

"Tactful as always," Henry said mildly.

"You know where you get it, Lucy," Donald said, punching his sister lightly on the arm to try and cheer her.

"Thanks, Donald," Lucy answered wanly. "Yeah, Mom, that about sums it up."

She turned to Sayesha. "So what should I do? If I go back and reverse this, I can save Scott, but then Dad dies, and we're back where we started."

"Remember, is not just your family. Is also a whole alien civilization, too," Sayesha said pointedly.

"You mean—oh yeah, the Akwatairs. If Dad's ship

hadn't exploded..."

"Since my ship never exploded, there was no wormhole created to travel through," Henry said slowly.

"And my ship didn't get lost..." Ellen added.

"So there was no rescue mission," interjected Dr. Hartwick with a catch in his voice.

"And I couldn't have led the Akwatairs to overthrow their government and save themselves. So, like a million people—aliens, whatever—are counting on me, too," Lucy concluded. "Time travel makes everything so complicated."

"Wait a minute." Lucy sat straight up in her chair. "The guy who set the bomb on Dad's ship was an Akwatair. He knew he had to do it so that I would end up on his planet!" Lucy cried.

"You mean," Donald began, then paused in confusion.

"Yes, Donald," Sayesha said calmly. "I see your mind, and you are being right." She smiled benignly at the faces that turned to her in astonishment. "Donald sees truth. The alien was also a time traveler, sent to make sure Lucy would still go to save Akwatair."

"It was OroLo," Lucy realized. "The Akwatair chief's son. I wasn't sure until now. I thought he was my friend, but he came back to kill my father."

"He is being your friend," Sayesha said. "And knowing you as a friend, he must have known you would find a solution for everyone."

Henry stood up suddenly. "You've got to let them destroy my ship, Lucy. If I live, an entire alien civilization will remain enslaved. I'll make the sacrifice for the greater good."

"No, you won't!" Ellen shouted, running to her husband and throwing her arms around him. "I don't care about some other planet. I care about you!"

Dr. Hartwick made a strangled sound. "I will take his place. Take me back in time, Lucy, and I will switch places with Henry."

"Oh my goodness, could you all stop being such heroes?" Lucy said in good-humored exasperation. "Dad, what if we let the bomb go off, but you and the crew get away in an escape pod just before it explodes? Then there'll still be a wormhole, and Mom's ship will still run into it."

"Perfect!" Donald whooped.

"But there is no escape pod," Henry said quietly. "Remember, the economy was struggling. Traveling on ships then was like traveling on the Titanic—not enough lifeboats." He paused. "And even if there were an escape pod, I doubt it could travel fast enough to get us safely away from the radiation."

A gloom settled over the company.

My dad or my boyfriend? Lucy thought, miserably. *And all the Akwatairs, too, but compared to those two... Of course, I should want it to be my dad who's saved. I'm such an awful person, I don't know what to think.*

Sayesha put an arm around Lucy. *You are not an awful person*, she said in a stern telepathic voice. *You are an extraordinary human being with normal, complex emotions.*

"We figure this out," Sayesha announced. "We just need time. So many genius brains here," she winked, "we must find a solution."

"Of course you're right, Sayesha," Ellen said gratefully. "Let's take a break, go for a walk, get back to work for a bit, or otherwise clear our minds. We'll let this problem percolate for a while in our heads. We're bound to come up with an answer."

There was grudging agreement as people began to stir from their seats.

"Wait!" Dr. Hartwick cried. "This resident genius brain has the answer." He tapped the side of his head, grinned, and winked at Sayesha.

"What is it, Dr. Hartwick?" asked Lucy.

"The alien spaceship," he answered simply. "That will be our escape pod."

"What do you mean?" asked Donald.

"I will take it back in time and insist that it be attached to the base of Henry's ship. There is a space to attach an escape pod, just no money for one," he explained.

"You have the kind of power that could force them to do that?" Lucy said dubiously.

Dr. Hartwick looked affronted. "I don't know what I

was like in that other universe of yours, Lucy," he said, "but in this one, yes, I wield considerable power. You will write a note, which I will give Henry and tell him not to open until after takeoff. The note will explain that he and the crew must evacuate the ship after it is launched and head forward to our time. The *Icarus* will still explode, no trace of the crew will be found, and Lucy will still head out to save her mother. And Lucy's young man will not die en route to defuse a bomb."

He beamed triumphantly at the group.

"That's perfect, Dr. Hartwick!" Lucy enthused.

"Wait," Donald interrupted. "What about you, Dr. Hartwick? How will you get home?"

Oh, crud, thought Lucy, *I'd forgotten about that.*

"I believe I have a solution," Dr. Hartwick answered thoughtfully. "The time loop Lucy used will be in place, right? And the time machine will still be waiting to re-enter the loop. I can come home in the old time machine."

There was a pause as everyone considered the plan.

Ellen finally broke the silence. "Won't the technicians working on the particle accelerator in the cave be surprised when a time machine shows up in the middle of the room?"

Lucy found herself giggling at the thought, and everyone joined in the laughter.

"You forgot just one thing, Dr. Hartwick," she said.

"What's that?" he asked in surprise.

"I'm going with you."

"And so am I," added Donald.

"No way," Ellen began to sputter.

"Forget it, Mom," Lucy said with a grin. "Don't you know me yet? I'll find a way, whether you want me to or not."

Ellen's face darkened, but Henry stepped in and laid a gentle hand on her shoulder.

"It's her adventure, Ellen. She's saved both of our lives once already. Better just go with it."

Ellen's shoulders slumped, and she nodded. "Okay, Lucy. But this is it, you got it?"

"Whatever you say, Mom."

Chapter 20

⚜ ⚜ ⚜

As the others stood up and headed toward the villa, Lucy tugged on Donald's sleeve to hold him back.

"What's up?" Donald asked, frowning.

"There's another problem that no one here knows about," Lucy whispered. She gulped and looked around nervously.

"I'm waiting," he said grimly.

"Remember how I said that the time loop was flickering off and on? And we actually fell out of it when we landed in Rome the second time?"

Donald crossed his arms over his chest and raised one eyebrow. "Are you trying to tell me it wasn't just a glitch in the system?"

"Yes. I felt funny telling the others this, but I think I actually heard Sayesha's voice in my head, calling to me through time. She was warning me. I think the lab was under attack, and that's why our travel was interrupted. The time loop is powered by antimatter, which is created by a particle accelerator. If someone sabotaged our power

246

source, the time loop will be gone. We won't be able to get home."

Donald paused to think. "Well, I guess we have to trust Dr. Hartwick and his team," he answered. "You said you left Mom a note explaining where you were going, right? If the time loop wasn't running, they'd know you were stuck in the past. Dr. Hartwick would repair the accelerator as quickly as possible."

"Can he even fix it?" Lucy asked anxiously. "Especially in an attack."

"I don't know, Lucy. But are you sure you weren't imagining things? I mean, you must have been stressed out. It's hard to believe that Sayesha could have contacted you from the future."

"I know it seems unlikely," she admitted. "And after all the trouble I had convincing everyone to believe in my time traveling, I didn't dare mention that, too. But Donald, the more I think about it, the more sure I am. Connecting with Sayesha again in this universe makes me certain that she has an important part to play in all this. Maybe that warning was part of it."

"Okay, just for the sake of argument, we'll assume she managed to contact you and warn you about some danger back home. But who would want to attack the villa?" demanded Donald.

"I don't know for sure. There had been a lot of threats against the time machine team, and Dr. Hartwick was worried that an enemy government, or maybe a terrorist group, would steal the time machine and use it against us. Dr. Hartwick said the time machine had to be destroyed. That's why Scott and I took off in the machine in such a hurry. And that's why I insisted on going with Dr. Hartwick now. I'm afraid, when he returns, he'll get caught in the middle of a firefight," she finished in a rush.

Donald stroked his chin thoughtfully, considering this information.

Scott does the same thing, Lucy realized in surprise as she watched her brother's absent-minded movement.

"Okay," Donald said. "I'm not sure if we could get hold of any guns, but at least I know karate. Mom sent you to a self-defense class, didn't she?"

Lucy felt relief flooding over her. "Yeah, I know a few moves."

Donald glanced down at Fido, rooting in the dirt near Lucy. "Plus, we've got a half-grown wolf on our side."

"Half-grown? What do you mean?" She turned to stare hard at Fido and exclaimed, "He really is bigger. A lot bigger!"

"Maybe time travel affects an animal's metabolism more than a human's," Donald said. "It could have aged him a little more."

"I wonder if he'll get younger when we go back again?"

"Time will tell," Donald said with a grin. He put up his fists in a mock fighting posture. "What do you say,

Luce? Shall we practice?"

"You're on," Lucy said good-naturedly as she rushed forward to tackle her brother.

Fido looked up with a growl, instantly aware of the scene. In a single, graceful leap, he pounced on Donald, knocking him to the ground. The wolf snarled and stretched his neck to reach for Donald's throat.

"Fido, no!" Lucy screamed. *Get off him*, she thought simultaneously.

Fido paused in confusion, and Donald quickly rolled out from under him and scrambled to his feet.

"I'm so sorry, Donald," she apologized. "He was just trying to protect me."

"That was awesome," Donald said.

"Almost getting your jugular ripped out was awesome?" Lucy asked in disbelief.

"Well, the way he wanted to protect you is pretty awesome, and so is the way he obeyed you. You'd never know he's a wild animal. I'm thinking that if we had a few days, we could train him as an attack dog."

Lucy nodded in agreement. "You're right! I'm sure we can stall Dr. Hartwick for awhile." She bent down to embrace Fido. "Maybe Sayesha is right about destiny. Maybe I was destined to find you so you could help us," she told the young wolf.

Lucy and Donald spent nearly a week training Fido, working in the fields behind the villa where they could practice undisturbed. A battered scarecrow inspired them to make a battalion of straw men that they trained Fido to attack. Lucy found that if she mixed verbal commands with mental images of what she wanted the wolf to do, Fido could usually understand and obey her. The first few scarecrows were mangled beyond recognition, but the wolf quickly learned control, so a real target would be disabled but not killed. After several days of training, Lucy and Donald decided to move on to a real target: Donald.

"Why did I agree to this?" Donald complained, looking down in dismay at his layers of shirts, coats and pants. "I'm so hot in all these layers!"

Lucy looked him over critically. "Quit whining, Don. Maybe you do look like a human marshmallow. But would you rather be too hot, or bitten to pieces by a wolf?"

"Well, when you put it that way..." Donald sheepishly agreed.

Lucy grinned back, then turned to give her wolf a quick pat.

"Okay, Fido, this is it. You've got a real person to practice on, not a scarecrow. Are you ready?"

Fido looked into Lucy's eyes, and she sensed his calm trust in her.

"Are you ready, too, Donald?" she called out.

"As ready as I'll ever be," he answered. "I hope a pair of jeans and two pairs of sweat pants are enough," he muttered to no one in particular.

250

A Doorway Through Time

Lucy laid a hand on Fido, closed her eyes and visualized him clenching Donald's leg in his powerful jaws.

"Fido, attack!" she cried aloud.

The wolf raced toward Donald and leaped. Donald braced himself, but he was no match for the speed and force of Fido's attack. Donald tumbled to the ground, and Fido quickly wrapped his teeth around Donald's leg, in the exact spot Lucy had pictured.

"Release!" she shouted.

Fido relinquished his hold on Donald and sat on his haunches. He whined and licked Donald's sneaker.

"I know you had to do what she said," Donald said to the wolf.

He reached down to scratch Fido under the chin. The wolf thumped his tail loudly on the ground and bared his teeth in a wolfish grin.

"Don't worry about it, Fido. In the end, we all have to obey her," Donald teased.

"Hmmph," Lucy snorted. "Come here, Fido, and I'll give you a treat. You okay, Donald?"

"He ripped through both layers of sweatpants, but I'm fine. I don't think his heart was really in it."

"As long as his heart is in it if we end up being attacked," she replied.

Donald watched thoughtfully as Fido gulped down his treat. "It's pretty impressive how he had such good control. It must have gone against all his instincts." He sighed dramatically. "I guess it must be my amazing training skills."

"Excuse me, it's my telepathic skills," Lucy retorted.

There was a rustling movement in the grass, and an alto voice interrupted the siblings.

"So you are being prophet now, Lucy? You see great battle coming you prepare for?"

"Sayesha?" Lucy asked guiltily. "Did you see it all? What are you doing out here?"

"Am wondering what you spend so much time doing. Now I be seeing. Why for you make dog bite Donald?"

Lucy took a deep breath. "I was going to tell you about this soon anyway, Sayesha, so it's just as well you saw us."

Use your mind, not your mouth, please, interrupted Sayesha telepathically.

I've heard that before, said Lucy ruefully. *From OroLo, that Akwatair I told you about. Okay, here's the problem.*

Lucy quickly explained the situation to Sayesha, who nodded gravely throughout the story.

Well, Lucy, Sayesha answered, *if I warned you the lab was being attacked, I must have been nearby. I would've felt your mind disappear when you traveled back through time, and I'm sure I would've contacted your family. Besides, if my Roland knew his lab was in danger, he would've taken precautions. He would do anything to protect you, Lucy... And so would I.*

"When you save Scott and the alien people," Sayesha

said aloud for Donald's benefit, "things may change again, who knows how? But you call to me through time, and I will hear you."

"Thank you so much, Sayesha," Lucy exclaimed in relief. "I feel way better now. I just know you're meant to help."

That night, Dr. Hartwick declared that they would depart in three days time. "We'll leave on Monday, my favorite day of the week. It's a good day to begin an adventure!"

"Monday? Really?" Lucy said in disbelief. "Only you, Dr. Hartwick."

Lucy, Donald, and Fido practiced steadily for the next few days until Monday finally arrived. Lucy, Donald, and Dr. Hartwick, loaded down with packs, climbed the hill to the ship, accompanied by Ellen, Henry, and Sayesha.

Ellen embraced her daughter fiercely. "Be careful, darling girl."

"I will," Lucy promised. "And, uh, you be careful, too, Mom."

Ellen looked strangely at her, but Lucy turned to embrace her father.

"Love you, Dad," she said with a catch in her voice.

"You, too, Lucy-bear," he whispered into her hair.

Lucy turned to Sayesha then. "Thank you—for everything," she said pointedly.

253

Sayesha smiled beatifically. "No worries, Lucy."

After all the good-byes were said, Lucy placed her palms on the ship to open the doors and led the men inside. Fido, however, refused to enter. He laid his ears back and whined unhappily.

"Fido's not really a fan of time travel," Lucy explained.

"Is there something we should know, Lucy?" asked Dr. Hartwick.

"Umm, well, it gets pretty hot, and you feel some pressure," she said equivocally.

Donald cocked his head quizzically. "Is that the truth, the whole truth, and nothing but the truth?"

"Okay, first you feel like you're going to melt, and then you think your guts are going to turn to mush," Lucy admitted. "But other than that, it's not too bad."

"Great," said Donald as he scooped up Fido with a grunt. "C'mon, wolf, you're with me."

Dr. Hartwick looked nervous but simply remarked, "I suppose this is the price I pay for science."

To Lucy's surprise, Sayesha leaned forward and gently stroked Dr. Hartwick's back. "That being my brave one," she said sweetly.

What the heck? Lucy wondered.

You left me alone quite a bit this week, Lucy, Sayesha explained. *Dr. Hartwick and I got to know each other better.*

Wow! That's great! So are you—

A Doorway Through Time

Not now. Go. Your adventure awaits. And then you must all come back safely to me. To all of us.

Lucy smiled and nodded. "Good-bye, everyone!" she called in what she hoped was an optimistic tone. As she stepped into the ship, however, a new worry struck her. "Gee, there's only two seats," she said. "I don't think you guys can double-buckle."

"Maybe there's a matching seat on the other side?" Donald suggested.

Lucy ran her hands along the other side of the ship and was relieved when another seat folded out from the wall. "Phew! Good thinking, Donald!"

She sank into the pilot's chair. "How about I drive?"

Dr. Hartwick raised his hands in the air. "I certainly don't want to drive it! I just want to understand how it works—eventually."

Donald nodded. "Okay with me, too."

"All right, then, watch the master." Lucy turned to the controls, deftly tapped in the date she and Dr. Hartwick had calculated earlier, and zoomed in on the map to select the space station in Florida again.

Donald gave a low whistle of admiration. "Very cool."

"Yes, it is," Lucy agreed as she started the ship and carefully headed up toward the clouds. "Hold on to Fido, and give him a pat for me, Donald," she called out. "This is where it gets really interesting."

Lucy was prepared for the familiar scorching birth

of the star, the intense pressure of the black hole, and the spinning glare of the white hole. The men, however, were not, and she listened to their gasps of astonished pain with sympathy.

"Don't worry, it's always like this," she managed to croak out.

Then it was over, and they were hurtling out from utter blackness to brilliant whiteness to the gray light of a misty Florida morning. Lucy fought to bring the ship under control, jamming on the brake as she spun the wheel counterclockwise to oppose its clockwise spin. At last, her efforts were rewarded as the ship shuddered and hung suspended in the air.

"Well, that was the worst ride ever," Donald finally managed to say. "But you did a good job handling the ship," he quickly added, seeing Lucy's stricken face.

"It's always awful," she agreed, somewhat mollified. "Fido had a hard time on the last trip. But you don't look too bad now, do you, Fido?"

Fido thumped his tail weakly, and Lucy turned her attention to Dr. Hartwick.

"Are you all right, Dr. Hartwick?"

He groaned a little and nodded in response.

"Okay then, down we go."

They hastily clambered out of the spaceship, and Lucy was relieved to see color returning to Dr. Hartwick's ashen face.

"Right, so the first stop is to find my younger self," said Dr. Hartwick, squinting as he got his bearings. "At this hour of the day, I should be in my office, making sure everything is ready for the launch. Let's hope I listen to reason!"

They took off toward the space center at a jog, Dr. Hartwick panting as he struggled to keep up. As they approached a side door, a security guard stepped out of the shadows.

"Halt! ID, please." The guard paused and stared, wide-eyed. "Dr. Hartwick? Didn't I just see you a few minutes ago in the cafeteria?"

"Yes, well, I headed outside, same as you. I, uh, forgot something in my hovercar. Now let me through, please. My guests, Lucy and Donald Starrett, have special clearance, like me."

"Yes sir, but the dog? He can't enter this building unless he's a service dog."

"Then he's a service dog," said Dr. Hartwick icily.

Way to go, Dr. Hartwick, thought Lucy in admiration.

"I don't see a special harness," the guard began.

There was a blur of movement, and the guard crumpled to the floor.

"Donald?" Lucy cried in amazement.

"Sorry," he apologized. "I think I punched him hard enough to put him out for awhile. C'mon, Lucy," he said, seeing her expression. "He was too suspicious, and we had to get going."

257

"I know, it's just that's more my line than yours," she said, still surprised.

Alter the space-time continuum a little, and people's personalities sure do change a lot, she mused.

Dr. Hartwick was staring at the guard in dismay and shaking his head. "What's done is done, I suppose," he finally said. "We'll have to hope his memory is cloudy when he wakes. Let's hide him someplace safe and get going."

Dr. Hartwick placed his hand on a scanner at the entrance, and the door clicked open.

"Drag him inside and leave him near the stairwell," he ordered.

Lucy and Donald each grabbed an arm and pulled the guard inside, Fido close at their heels.

"And that's how aliens slip right in and plant bombs," Dr. Hartwick muttered as they hurried down the antiseptic hallways. "Terrible security. Ah, there I am!"

At the end of the hall, Lucy made out the large, dark figure of Dr. Hartwick holding a gigantic mug of coffee in one hand and two doughnuts in the other.

"Hello, Dr. Hartwick!" Lucy shouted.

The figure turned and stopped in shocked disbelief.

"How? Who?" stammered the younger version of Dr. Hartwick.

"Yes, I'm you! From the future!" began the older Dr. Hartwick.

"This is impossible," the younger Dr. Hartwick said

faintly.

"That's where you're—I'm—wrong. You're here, I'm here, so obviously it is possible. I'm you from the future. I see you had the foresight to get two doughnuts, one for each of us. Unless you'd like to share?" he asked, suddenly remembering Donald and Lucy.

The teenagers shook their heads.

"What's my middle name?" demanded the younger Dr. Hartwick.

"Obediah," the older Dr. Hartwick replied. "We hate that name and have never told anyone what it is."

"What was the name of my boyhood pet?"

"It was a tortoise named Philip."

"What's my favorite color?"

"You—I—don't have a favorite color."

"You *are* me!" exclaimed the younger Dr. Hartwick in excitement. "And Lucy and Donald are looking—well, a little older, I suppose. Why are you here?"

The older Dr. Hartwick quickly explained the situation and what they needed to do to set things right. The younger Dr. Hartwick listened intently.

"You're sure about this?" asked the younger Dr. Hartwick.

"Quite. It's the only way."

"I wish there were time for me to examine your ship," said the younger Dr. Hartwick wistfully. "But we must go immediately. I will make sure that the alien craft is attached to the base of the ship. And Lucy, I'll give the note to your father."

"Make sure my dad understands he mustn't open it until after take-off," Lucy added anxiously.

"Don't worry, my dear," the younger Dr. Hartwick said kindly. "And this note of yours explains not just why he must evacuate the ship, but also how to operate the alien pod?"

"Yes, I went over it three times," Lucy affirmed. "Thank you so much."

"You know I'd do anything to protect your family, Lucy."

The younger Dr. Hartwick leaned over and gave his older self a pat on the belly.

"Still eating plenty of doughnuts even in the future, I see! Some things never change!"

"Indeed they don't. Well, good luck, me!" called the older Dr. Hartwick. "I can't believe I just insulted myself," he said in a low voice as he turned to go.

Lucy giggled. "You look just fine, Dr. Hartwick. I know Sayesha thinks so, too."

Dr. Hartwick's face softened. "So she does."

"Guys? We have a plane to catch," Donald interrupted.

They hurried then, bustling down the corridor and catching a shuttle to the nearest airport. After presenting their credentials, and after Fido was scanned to ensure the authorities of his good health, they were finally in the air, winging their way to Rome. When they landed, Dr. Hartwick left to secure hoverbus tickets to Silvano. Lucy saw Donald transfixed by a large news monitor.

"It's Muffy Robertson," he breathed, "reporting on Dad's ship."

Apparently Donald has a crush on that newscaster in every universe, thought Lucy in disgust.

"Should I leave you two alone, or can I watch, too?"

"Shhh!" chided Donald.

"For our viewers who are just joining us, the spaceship *Icarus* has just taken off on its journey to Mars. It will deliver important supplies to further the growth of the colony on the red planet. The president has supported this mission from the start, saying—wait a moment." Muffy Robertson looked momentarily confused. "Sources say that the escape pod, which was just attached today, a last-minute donation from an anonymous benefactor, has separated from the ship."

"Look, Donald!" cried Lucy. "Do you see that bright light in the background? Dad's started up the time machine. The star is beginning to form."

"It is unclear whether or not the crew is on board the pod," Muffy continued. "What is certain is that alarms are going off, and there seems to be some problem on board the *Icarus*."

"The star's gone," Donald whispered. "It must have collapsed and made the black hole."

261

Judith Bourassa Joy

Suddenly, before their eyes, the *Icarus* exploded in a giant mushroom cloud of deadly energy. Lucy fought back tears as she watched the devastation.

"That's what killed Dad the first time," she choked out.

"But not this time," Donald said firmly. "You can trust Dad to have gotten the pod into the black hole before the ship blew."

Lucy took a deep, shuddering breath. "You're right, things are different this time," she agreed. "And that means Scott is still alive, too!" she rejoiced. "There will still be a wormhole for Mom's ship to go through, and we'll still go to Tairran to rescue her and save the innocent Akwatairs from their awful government."

Fido, who had been whining during the newscast, suddenly broke into a howl at Dr. Hartwick's feet.

"Hush, Fido!" Lucy said gently. "Everything's going to be all right now."

She glanced at Dr. Hartwick and was overwhelmed by a sudden sense of foreboding. She drew Fido to her and buried her face in his warm fur, wanting Donald to think she was comforting the pup, not herself.

"I hope," she whispered.

Chapter 21

It was midnight by the time Lucy, Donald, and Dr. Hartwick made their weary way back to the villa. They had spent the night cajoling suspicious customs officials at the airport to allow Fido into the country, enduring a crowded, uncomfortable trip via hoverbus to Silvano, and unable to find a taxi at that late hour, taking a labored hike up the winding road. The villa was dark and quiet, its inhabitants presumably asleep.

Dr. Hartwick pulled a heavy iron key from his pocket. "Let's hope the lock is the same," he murmured.

He inserted the key into the ornate keyhole, and to Lucy's relief, the key turned easily. Dr. Hartwick gave the door a push, and it swung open, hinges creaking. Lucy looked around anxiously, but the foyer was silent and empty. She pulled out a flashlight from her pack and turned it on, carefully shining the light straight down on the floor.

"We have to hope no one sees us," Lucy said in a low voice.

She glanced wistfully down the hallway that would lead to her living quarters, once she returned to her own time.

I wonder where Scott is now, she thought.

"Of course, the big question is, are they using the cavern?" Donald whispered as they hurried down the hallway to the lab.

"And if they are using the cavern, did they leave the time machine alone?" added Dr. Hartwick.

They reached the lab entrance, and after a moment's hesitation, Dr. Hartwick turned the door handle. They were greeted by the familiar sight of the lab, complete with banks of computers humming quietly.

"So far, so good," Lucy murmured. She tiptoed over to the door that, in her own time, led to the cavern elevator. She angled the flashlight's beam inside and saw the familiar broom cupboard, filled with cleaning implements. "It's the same security hologram!" she crowed.

Lucy stepped forward confidently, and there was a loud crash as brooms and dustpans came clattering down.

"Ow! What the—" Lucy sputtered. "That's no hologram!"

"That answers our question, anyway," Donald said with a chuckle. "It means the time machine will be waiting for us, untouched."

Their relief faded instantly, however, as an alarm sounded and all the lights in the villa came on.

"Aw, crud, we've got to get out of here, fast," Lucy

growled. "C'mon!"

The three of them spun around and ran for the door, Fido at their heels. As they raced down the hallway to the main entrance, Lucy could hear the sound of footsteps in pursuit. She looked back and recognized the cook, holding a heavy frying pan as a weapon. "Renata?" Lucy began, quickly realizing that the woman would have no idea yet who she was. Renata stopped momentarily in confusion.

Lucy didn't dare pause any longer but rushed out the main door after the men. They didn't stop running until they were well up the hill, hidden in the brush. Dr. Hartwick sat down heavily, panting and sweating profusely.

"Do you think they'll follow us?" Donald asked.

"I hope not," Lucy replied. "I don't think Renata will chase after us, but she might call the police." She glanced down at Dr. Hartwick's recumbent figure. "We should get going as soon as we're able."

"You mean as soon as I'm able," Dr. Hartwick wheezed. He pulled a water bottle from his pack and took a long swig. "Just a few more minutes, please."

Lucy sank to the ground with her back against an olive tree. Fido stretched out next to her and lay his head on her lap. Moments later, the wolf was snoring contentedly. Lucy smiled wanly and wearily stroked his head. Donald sat nearby, and Lucy watched as his head repeatedly drooped down and jerked up again as he fought off waves of sleep.

A few minutes later, Donald lapsed into slumber.

Maybe I can just rest my eyes for a minute, too, and then get everyone going, Lucy decided.

Lucy closed her eyes and, without meaning to, quickly drifted off to sleep. Her dreams were troubled, though, filled with images from her travels—of Romi and Remi in ancient Rome, and Remi's stricken face as she left them behind. She dreamed that Remi spoke to her.

"Don't forget, Lucy," he pleaded. "Convince Mother— and Father—to join us here."

"I won't forget!" Lucy called.

Donald woke with a start. "Lucy, why did you shout 'I won't forget' just now?" He looked up at the pale sky, faintly pink with the coming dawn. "Oh man, we slept a long time."

Lucy rubbed her eyes and looked over at Dr. Hartwick. He was curled on the ground in a fetal position, snoring.

"I was dreaming about Romi and Remi," she said in a strained voice. "Remi, mostly. He was being brave, but I think he really wanted his parents to join him in ancient Rome. We've got to convince them to go back in time."

"I have a lot of trouble seeing Uncle Marcus agree to that," Donald said dubiously. "But one thing at a time, Lucy. Our cousins may not even be in ancient Rome if we don't wrap up this adventure!"

"You're right," she agreed. "Let's wake up Dr. Hartwick and get going."

A Doorway Through Time

Somewhat refreshed from their naps, they made good progress up the hill. Lucy soon found the fissure in the cliff that led to the underground tunnel, and they squeezed through. After a long march downhill, with only twinkling flashlights to pierce the absolute blackness, they finally reached the cavern. A pulsing glow of light welcomed them.

"Yes!" Dr. Hartwick shouted, as Lucy and Donald whooped in delight. Fido ran circles around them, sensing their excitement.

"The time loop is on!" Lucy exclaimed. "Guess you were right," she whispered as she hugged Donald with relief. "Good old Dr. Hartwick. That means the time machine must be..." She swung the flashlight in crazy arcs, lighting up the opaque stalactites and stalagmites. "Right here!" The beam of light came to rest on the erie outline of the time machine pod.

They rushed to the pod, then stopped short in dismay.

"It looks terrible," Donald said.

The machine was coated in thick dust, but a thin layer of orange rust and dark, oxidized blotches showed through the grime.

"It is 2,000 years old at this point," Dr. Hartwick reminded them.

"Think the warranty's expired?" Donald joked grimly.

Lucy hesitated. "The closed time loop provides the power. This pod is just a vessel to enter the loop safely."

She paused to think. "But we do have to start the engine to slip into and out of the loop, so let's give it a try," Lucy said with more assurance than she felt.

The door to the pod reluctantly slid open and they stepped inside. Lucy sat down at the controls and pressed the Power button. To her enormous relief, the pod lights turned on and the dashboard came to life.

"Your engineers in my timeline did good work, Dr. Hartwick," she said happily. "It still starts after all these years!"

Lucy programmed in the target date of July 31, 2065, AD. She pressed the Enter button, but there was no response from the pod engine. She tried again and again, and still nothing happened.

What are we going to do? she thought in panic. *Are we going to be stuck in this time forever, hiding from our other selves?*

She looked around at the others, and from the expressions on their faces, she knew they were having similar thoughts.

She grimaced. "I guess I spoke too soon."

"Maybe not," Donald said thoughtfully. "We know there's still a power source because the lights came up. It must have something to do with the ignition. I think we should crack this thing open and take a look."

Dr. Hartwick looked excited. "I don't do much hands-on work anymore, but between the two of us, I bet we can figure it out!"

Lucy smoothed out a spot on the ground to watch and wait as the two men located an access panel and peeled back a layer of the pod's metal skin. Lucy and Fido curled up companionably together on the cave floor and snacked some more as they waited for news. Finally, Donald and Dr. Hartwick stood up, brushed off their clothes, and reattached the access panel.

"Well...?" Lucy probed.

Donald turned to her with a smile. "We cleaned up some corrosion and tightened all the connections. There were a few frayed wires that we fixed, too."

"Took me way back to my early college years," Dr. Hartwick commented. "It was quite fun, actually!"

"Okay, guys," Lucy said, rising. "Let's see if you solved the problem."

They entered the pod and Lucy turned the power back on. Again, the dashboard lit up, and again, she programmed in the date.

"And now for the moment of truth," she said grimly. She reached for the Enter button and pushed it, her hand shaking slightly. Nothing happened. She pushed it again, but still nothing happened.

"One more time," Donald said in a strained voice.

Lucy drew a deep breath and pressed the button firmly. There was a grinding noise, a metallic thump, and then the familiar throb of the engine filled the room.

"Third time's the charm," Lucy mumbled, fighting back tears as she recalled Scott's last words.

"Let's strap in, Donald!" Dr. Hartwick cried happily.

The pod jerked forward and stopped abruptly. There was a new sound now as the engine noise grew louder and more insistent.

"Are we stuck?" Donald asked incredulously.

"It does rather seem that way," Dr. Hartwick replied, frowning.

"What am I supposed to do?" Lucy cried. "I can't stop the machine once it's started."

To everyone's surprise, the pod seemed to sense its own failure to launch. The display went black. Immediately, the engine cut out and the unnerving sound disappeared. The pod's door automatically unlocked, and they all scrambled out.

"Oh, I see," Lucy breathed, nodding in understanding as she scanned the base of the pod. It was embedded in gravel, and near the back, drips from overhead stalactites had formed piles of hardened minerals against the sides. "How did we miss that before?"

Donald was kneeling, chipping at the encrusted line of minerals.

"It's built up at least six inches," he called. "No wonder we couldn't move it!"

"Oh brother," Lucy said. "It's like backing the hovercar into a snowbank back home. Time to push it out!"

A Doorway Through Time

They all leaned on the back of the pod and shoved. It refused to budge. They tried pushing from different angles, in different positions but made no headway.

"What if we had the engine going when we pushed?" Donald suggested. "Maybe that would give us the edge we need."

"The door automatically shuts and locks when you start up the pod," Lucy objected.

"Yes, but..." Dr. Hartwick paused. "We could jam it."

He strode into the pod and began tugging at an arm on the captain's chair.

"Donald, if you please?" he called.

The two men managed to break off an arm, which Donald placed horizontally in the doorframe.

"Whoever pushes this pod out of the rock is going to have to jump in once it gets going," he pointed out.

"Then I will sit at the controls, since I doubt I would succeed at making a running leap back into the pod," Dr. Hartwick said quickly.

"I'm a klutz," Lucy said. "But I'll help you, Don."

Once Dr. Hartwick was settled at the wheel, Lucy and Donald stood at the back of the pod and leaned hard on it. Fido, who refused to stay in the pod, whined anxiously nearby.

"You could push, too, you know," Lucy growled good-naturedly at him. To her surprise, the wolf joined her, rearing up on his hind legs and placing his front legs on the pod.

"Okay, that's pretty weird," Lucy said aloud. "Uh, thanks, Fido."

Lucy, Donald, and Fido leaned on the craft again with all their weight. The engine rumbled to life. There was a crash as the pod door failed to shut, thwarted by the broken chair arm, followed by a scraping sound as the pod slowly began inching forward.

"All right, we've got it started," Donald gasped. "Keep going!"

Lucy pushed and strained as the pod continued its slow forward motion. Sweat streamed down her forehead, and her muscles burned as she put all her strength into her labors. Lucy was beginning to despair of ever reaching the time loop when she realized the pod was sliding more easily. She looked over at Donald.

"It's starting to feel the pull of the loop," he affirmed. "Let's give it one last big push and hop on."

They both leaned hard on the pod, and it quickly slipped forward.

"Hurry!" Lucy shouted.

She and Donald sprinted to catch the pod, Fido bounding ahead. The wolf leaped effortlessly aboard, and Donald jumped in after him. Lucy was about to climb in when her foot caught on a small boulder and she stumbled.

"Donald!" she shrieked.

A Doorway Through Time

Donald reached out and pulled her in just as the nose of the pod entered the loop. Lucy quickly pulled the broken chair arm from the track of the door. A blast of heat assaulted her as the pod door slammed shut.

"Are you okay?" Donald asked anxiously.

Lucy nodded. "Luckily, I'm fine. Ready to fight."

"What do you mean, 'fight'?" Dr. Hartwick asked sharply.

Lucy turned guiltily toward him. "There may be some kind of assault on the villa when we return. People may be trying to steal the time machine."

"Now you tell me?" Dr. Hartwick shouted in consternation.

Before he could say more, however, the pod stopped abruptly and began sliding back.

Lucy concentrated hard. *Sayesha, if you can hear me, we're arriving in the time machine. I hope you're ready.* "We're here," Lucy said unnecessarily.

The sharp staccato of rapid gunfire underscored the shouts and curses of men speaking in a foreign language.

"We're definitely not alone," Lucy said. "Time for battle."

Chapter 22

꙳ ꙳ ꙳

Lucy was startled by a rap on the pod door. She opened it cautiously to find her brother and Dr. Hartwick. "Huh? How did you get out there?"

Donald answered, "Dr. Hartwick just got the time loop running. Sayesha told me you were on your way back, so we hurried down here to meet you."

Lucy's head spun as she tried to make sense of things. "But you were time traveling with me!"

"No, Lucy, I just got to Italy from my summer internship. Mom panicked after you took off in Dr. Hartwick's time machine, and then suddenly Dad and his crew showed up in an alien spaceship. You have a lot of explaining to do!"

Dr. Hartwick nodded. "I did my best to tell your family what you told me when you traveled back in time to save your father. I knew that people would be unlikely to believe me. I was half-convinced I'd gone mad myself. And I knew I shouldn't alter the future any more than you'd intended."

A Doorway Through Time

Lucy blinked uncertainly. "This is too weird." She raced to the cupboard at the back of the pod and began tearing through the boxes of supplies.

"What are you doing?" Donald cried. "We need to get out of here!"

"I know, but I'm sure there must be more knives or something that the scientists stocked for their time travel costumes." Lucy was dumping out boxes unceremoniously when she shouted in triumph. "Score! I found two Roman swords."

She handed one to Donald and lightly held the other in her right hand, testing its weight. "It's a lot bigger and heavier than the ones we used to fence with in gym class," she said, "but it feels really well balanced."

"Balanced or not, here we come," Donald quipped as he gripped his sword and strode out of the pod into the glass tube that contained the time machine. He lifted the hatch in the floor and jumped down into the black base of the machine.

Lucy leaned out of the pod doorway and scanned the chaotic scene before her. Machinery was smashed and smoking. Warriors on both sides had fallen, some writhing in pain while others lay frighteningly still. Figures in blue uniforms were exchanging gunfire with hooded terrorists so completely clothed in black that it was impossible to tell if they were men or women.

Thank goodness the Italian police got involved, Lucy

thought to herself.

"Fido!" Lucy called aloud. The wolf ran to her side. "We fight together."

Lucy and Fido followed Donald down into the black base and out into the fray. Lucy paused for a moment, surprised by the sudden assault of sound. There was a smell of scorched skin and blood that made her nose wrinkle in distaste.

She put one hand on the wolf's head, then closed her eyes and visualized Fido attacking the men in dark clothing while protecting the uniformed police. When she opened her eyes, Fido had his eyes fixed on her, quivering in anticipation.

Lucy caught sight of a man in black, hidden behind a stalagmite and shooting any police officers who came within range.

"Attack," she whispered to the wolf, pointing at the sniper. In her mind, Lucy pictured Fido clutching the man by the throat.

Soundlessly, the wolf swept forward and pounced on the unsuspecting terrorist. There was a sickening crack, and the man gave a strangled cry and fell back, unconscious.

Eww, I didn't mean you should break his neck, Lucy thought unhappily.

In her moment of distraction, another black-suited man rushed at her from the side. Lucy saw the movement out of the corner of her eye and instinctively swung her sword. The man cried out in agony as the blade sliced his arm, and his laser gun tumbled to the ground.

"Sorry, but you asked for it," Lucy half-apologized.

She flipped the sword around and cracked the hilt against the man's head. With a groan, he lapsed into unconsciousness. Lucy scrambled for his dropped pistol.

"This is more like it," she murmured in satisfaction as she set the laser to stun.

Lucy continued to wage war, with Fido serving alternately as protector and attacker. The wolf was able to blend into the shadows and take terrorists by surprise, snapping arms and hands to prevent them from using their guns. Lucy followed suit, using her gun to stun long-range targets and the hilt of her sword to deliver more concussions to short-range targets. After several minutes of this, she felt a strong sense of horror emanating from Donald, and she scanned the melee, searching for her brother. She finally spotted him across the cavern, holding a terrorist by the shoulder as a human shield. The man, however, lay limp and bleeding.

Those jerks killed their own man so Donald couldn't use him as a shield, she realized. *This is no band of brothers—these are just mercenaries.*

A war whoop sounded behind her, and Lucy spun around to see Dr. Hartwick crowing triumphantly. He held the broken chair arm aloft, a terrorist crumpled at his feet.

"Way to go, Dr. Hartwick!" Lucy shouted.

Judith Bourassa Joy

There was a flash of light, and Dr. Hartwick's smile faded quickly as he collapsed on the floor of the cave. A dark stain quickly spread against his shirt.

"Dr. Hartwick!" Lucy shrieked.

She and Fido fought their way back to the time machine, waging unrelenting battle against the dark-robed men who were now converging on them. Lucy sensed Donald nearby and knew the remaining Italian policemen were doing their best to help. Lucy's grief and anger took over any rational thought, and she swung the sword recklessly in her left hand, shooting the pistol with her right. Fido remained by her side, snarling and ruthlessly attacking the enemy as they fought their way forward.

Numbers on both sides were dwindling, and the terrorists seemed to sense that victory was not necessarily theirs. One man, larger than the rest, called out in a harsh gutteral language. The other terrorists began to fall in, running back-to-back and circling the base of the time machine.

They look like a herd of bison, and they're probably a lot dumber, Lucy thought dismissively. *Well, it's not their machine and it never will be!*

There was a low groan, and Lucy's attention was drawn to Dr. Hartwick, who lay immobile near the time machine. The huge terrorist leader gave a short laugh and kicked Dr. Hartwick—hard.

Lucy was overwhelmed with anger. She flung the sword with all her strength, and it flew through the air, spinning. It found its target and sliced through the belly of the leader, skewering him to the side of the machine. Chaos ensued as the other terrorists, confused by the loss of their leader, broke ranks and scattered. The police, Donald, Lucy, and Fido took advantage of the confusion to methodically pick off the terrorists, one by one. Lucy had no sense of fatigue, thirst, or pain, as she hacked and shot her way through the crowd.

And then it was over. Utter silence descended on the cavern. Moments later, a new wave of sound engulfed them as the Italian police began spontaneously cheering.

"Yes! We did it!" Lucy cheered along with the others.

Fido whined suddenly, and Lucy remembered Dr. Hartwick. Together, they ran to the spot where Dr. Hartwick lay bleeding. His eyes had rolled up in his head, and he was completely limp. The side of his neck fluttered, however, in a very faint pulse.

If he's going to have any chance of surviving, I've got to stop the bleeding, Lucy thought.

She laid her hands over his wound and applied as much pressure as she dared.

"Somebody get help!" she shouted. "Dr. Hartwick's dying!"

Sayesha, where are you? Lucy shouted telepathically.

The next few minutes were a blur as the police radioed for help and left the cavern to join their comrades in the fighting above ground. Lucy and Donald bundled

Judith Bourassa Joy

Dr. Hartwick into the elevator and ascended to the surface. The elevator doors opened onto the smoking lab, which was littered with detritus from the fight. With a flash of color, Sayesha leaned down to help Lucy slide Dr. Hartwick out of the elevator.

"Oh, my dear one," Sayesha said softly as she stroked his pale face. "You are not long for this world, I think."

"No!" Lucy cried desperately. "No, Dr. Hartwick, I will go back in time again and change things so you don't get hurt!"

Dr. Hartwick's eyelids fluttered and opened. Blood bubbled from his lips as he struggled to focus his eyes on Sayesha.

"My new love," he murmured.

Sayesha smiled, but a tear escaped from her eye and rolled down her broad cheek. "In every time and for all time," she said.

Dr. Hartwick turned his bloodshot gaze to Lucy.

"Lucy. No more time travel. I see now. Someone must die. Let it be me. This time, let me save your family."

He coughed again, and blood gushed from his mouth.

"You see truly, my wise one," Sayesha said lovingly.

"The machine," he whispered, "must be destroyed. Sayesha—my pocket?"

Sayesha reached into his pants pocket and pulled out a small, oval-shaped device, black with a raised, red button in the center. She placed it gently in his hand.

A Doorway Through Time

"Love you," he whispered.

With a mighty effort, Dr. Hartwick squeezed his hand. There was a deafening roar, like the sound of a tidal wave crashing to shore. The villa's walls shuddered, and the floor rocked, but the building held firm.

Dr. Hartwick's eyes rolled back in his head, and Sayesha gently closed his eyelids.

"He is gone," Sayesha whispered as she leaned forward to kiss his forehead.

"What just happened?" Donald cried out in confusion.

Lucy looked into Sayesha's mind, which was laid bare for her.

"The time machine!" Lucy exclaimed in horrified understanding. "He set off the antimatter and destroyed the cavern!"

"He was being both wise and brave," Sayesha said solemnly.

Lucy buried her grimy face in her blood-soaked hands and wept.

Chapter 23

With Donald's help, Lucy made her way to her room and collapsed on the bed in exhaustion. Hours later, after she had finally managed to shower and dress, there was a soft tap on the door.

"Lucy?" called a familiar voice.

"Scott!" Lucy shrieked in delight.

She swung open the door and saw Scott standing there, a bandage wrapped around his handsome head and a wide grin on his face. Wordlessly, they fell into each other's arms while Fido growled softly and paced nearby.

"You're hurt!" Lucy cried once she emerged from their embrace.

"It's no big deal," Scott said, shrugging.

"What happened? Where were you?" she asked.

"It started upstairs," Scott explained. "I was busy fighting a group in the foyer with your mom, when a bunch of them split off and headed for the lab, and I guess they found their way to the cavern, too. Your mom had a little trouble, and I couldn't leave her. It sounds like you and Donald handled things pretty well underground, though."

"Well, we did have some help from the Italian police," Lucy admitted with a grin. "And Fido here was awesome. But I wouldn't say we did very well. After all, Dr. Hartwick..." her voice trailed off.

"I know, sweetheart," Scott said sympathetically, and he drew her into an embrace.

They stayed locked in each other's arms for several minutes while Lucy tried valiantly to compose herself.

"I'm okay," she said.

"Everyone's meeting in the library to debrief now," Scott told her. "Are you good to go?"

"Of course," Lucy affirmed. "We're together again."

With a sudden cry, she wrapped her arms again around Scott. "I couldn't bear it when you didn't survive in that other space-time. It was like I couldn't breathe."

"I can only imagine," Scott said softly, stroking her hair. Lucy clung to him for several long moments, then reluctantly broke away.

"Now I'm really ready."

As they entered the library, Lucy took quick stock of the people gathered there. To her surprise, her Uncle Marcus and Aunt Rhea sat stiffly on the window seat. Sayesha was in a rocking chair in the corner, rocking slowly and rhythmically. Donald was stretched in an armchair and Lucy's parents were together on the couch.

"Dad!" Lucy cried out. "You made it! You're alive!"

"I am indeed—thanks to you," Henry exclaimed, rising to embrace his daughter. "And so are the rest of the *Icarus* crew. They agreed to come to the future with me, knowing it was the only way to save the alien race responsible for the pod."

Their joyful reunion was interrupted, however, by a sharp voice from behind.

"So here you are, the girl who caused all this trouble and lost my boys!"

Lucy swiveled to face her uncle, who had risen from the window seat and now stood, red-faced and agitated. Rhea remained seated, her face strained with grief.

"My sons," Rhea said with heartbreaking simplicity. "Where are my boys?"

A wave of emotion engulfed Lucy, and she rushed to hug her aunt.

"Oh, Aunt Rhea," Lucy said softly, "that is a very long story."

"I have all night."

The dark night sky had grown pale in the light of a new dawn by the time Lucy, Scott, and Donald were finished telling their tales and Lucy had shown her photos to Marcus and Rhea.

"So my boys are responsible for founding Rome," Marcus said proudly. "I told you they'd amount to something, Rhea."

A Doorway Through Time

"They can't do it alone," Rhea said suddenly. "They need us. Remi asked for us."

She turned her lovely face to Henry. "The time machine you people made may have been destroyed in the explosion, but there is still that alien ship you used to escape with your crew."

Rhea rose and stood proudly, her figure statuesque and imposing, emanating an authority Lucy had never seen before.

"You owe it to us. You must give us the ship so that Marcus and I can go to our sons."

"But Aunt Rhea, they refused to leave. They—they wanted to oversee the founding of Rome, and if you bring them home, who knows what will happen to our history," Lucy objected.

"I never said anything about bringing them home," Rhea replied quietly. "I am going to live with them and help them. Marcus will come, too. His engineering skills will help the boys."

"I will?" Marcus gasped in surprise.

Rhea cast him a withering look.

"Yes, of course I will," he agreed meekly.

"You're right," Henry said finally. "It's too dangerous to fool with time and keep the machine here. Don't you think so, too, Ellen?"

"Yes," she agreed. "Rhea, you and Marcus deserve to take the alien ship back to your sons—as long as you agree to destroy the ship once you get there."

"Of course," Rhea said simply.

"But wait, first we have to use it to save Dr. Hartwick!" Lucy interjected.

"No, Lucy," Sayesha interrupted, speaking for the first time. "Roland Hartwick say no, and Sayesha Herero say no. There being something in this time that say someone must die. If the universe balanced, someone must die. First it was being your papa. Then Scott. Now Roland. Let it stay Roland. He was being ready."

Dr. Hartwick is gone from this world, but you will see him again someday, Lucy, Sayesha continued. *It is a thin membrane that separates the temporal from the eternal.*

"So we just give up?" Lucy choked out. She glanced around the room despairingly and saw her father, Scott, and Donald nodding.

"Not give up, Lucy," Sayesha said gently. "Just let go. You no failure. No failure at all. You save aliens, you save family, you save balance in universe. You save us all."

Lucy looked around at her family and friends, silently considering Sayesha's words.

"I don't know what to say," Lucy ventured. "Right now I just want to be grateful that Scott and Dad are alive. And Aunt Rhea and Uncle Marcus, I'm so glad that you will see your boys again."

With a small cry, Rhea and Ellen rose together and moved to Lucy, embracing her. The others joined them one

A Doorway Through Time

by one, and even Fido pushed his way into the circle. When the sun finally rose on that August morning, it shone down on a family united in time.

☥ ☥ ☥